Feather Woman of the Jungle

Best wishes

Harry

Signed by Harry the Hawk 3-8-95 Atlanta, GA

Feather Woman of the Jungle

Amos Tutuola

City Lights Books
San Francisco

First published by City Lights Books in 1988

Cover painting "The Anti-Bird Ghost" by Twins Seven Seven courtesy of Twins Seven Seven

Cover design: Patricia Fujii

Library of Congress Cataloging-in-Publication Data

Tutuola, Amos.
Feather woman of the jungle.

I. Title.
PR9387.9.T8F43 1988 823 88-1050
ISBN 0-87286-215-1

City Lights Books are available to bookstores through our primary distributor: Subterranean Company, P.O. Box 10233, Eugene, OR 97440 (503)343-6324. Our books are also available through library jobbers and regional distributors. For personal orders and catalogs, please write to City Lights Books, 261 Columbus Avenue, San Francisco CA 94133.

CITY LIGHTS BOOKS are edited by Lawrence Ferlinghetti and Nancy J. Peters and published at the City Lights Bookstore, 261 Columbus Avenue, San Francisco CA 94133.

Contents

Contents

The Biography of my Town in Brief

In eighteenth century, the hunter who first came to Abeokuta (Nigeria), emigrated in a few family and detachments and settled in a place called Abeokuta, just to save themselves from the wild beasts, and many other reasons. These emigrants are now known to be EGBA tribes, and the head and leader of these emigrants was ODUDUWA, a title. Oduduwa was the hero father of Yorubas. Of course, Egba people did not live together as they do now and they were very few.

Type of houses built: The houses were of mud and the roofs were thatched with grass and broad leaves, of course, these type of houses are still existing throughout the Yoruba villages.

The compounds were in form of square and every compound contained shrines of many gods to which the family sacrificed.

Daily tasks: Hardly in the morning when the day's tasks began, the spinners would take up their spindles, the weavers would take up their shuttles, the farmers would take up their hoes, cutlasses, etc., the warriors would take up their weapons, the drummers would take up their drums and the hunters would take up their bows and arrows.

Tribal marks: The tribal marks were different types and this was according to the choice of a family.

Women's dresses: The women's dresses were aprons, head ties, veils for young ladies or newly married ladies and top covers for old and married women only. Precious beads always on wrists, necks and waists. The camwood powder was used to rub the body and antimony for the eyelids.

Plays and amusements: Our plays and amusements were fables, folk-lores, proverbs, riddles, etc. etc., after day's work was over.

Means of communications to our neighbours or friends who were far off from us: Long, long ago, before the Yoruba people had ever dreamed of the white people and as there was no book knowledge, the Egba people had the means of communications by means of symbols which we used as letters and some of them are as follows—If two cowries were tied together faced each other, meant, "I want to see you". But if a long feather was added in return, it meant "be expecting me". If two cowries were tied back to back meant, "I shun you away". If another cowrie was added in return, it meant, "I kick you off". But if the coal was sent in return, it meant, "I fail to understand the cause of shunning me away". Etc., etc.

Believes: Many wild bushes were reserved or untouched simply not to drive away the spirits who were lurking in there. Mighty trees around the town were reserved as they were the inhabitations of spirits and witches.

All these things are still existing but are gradually dying.

Feather Woman of the Jungle

The Night Entertainments

When I was seventy-six years old, the chief of my village died. But as I was the oldest man in the village that time, therefore, I was chosen by the rest people in the village to be their new chief.

After the sixth month that I had become the chief, and as my people were always anxious to hear my past adventures before I had become a rich man. Therefore, one night, I invited all the people to my house. All sat in front of my house. The women sat in the left of the circle while the men sat in the right and I sat on my usual old high armchair a little distance in front of them. Then I supplied each of the people with a keg of palm-wine, and the biggest keg was in front of me.

As this time was a dry season, so the people could see me well and I could see them well also through the clear full moon of that dry season. But as the people were anxious greatly to hear the story very soon, they could not drink their palm-wine so much when one of them stood up and said loudly—"Yes, we are ready now to hear your adventures!" They thought that it was a story which could be related in one night but it was a great wonder to them at last to see that it took me several nights to relate the whole of it to the end. So this was the first night that the entertainments of my adventures began as follows.

The Witch of the Jungle

The entertainment of the first night

(*My first Journey*)

Now, my people, I am very glad indeed that you are anxious to hear the story of my past adventures, and I will start to tell you the story as from this night. But I advise every one of you to pay attention to it so that you may be able to sort out the useful senses which, I believe, will be useful to you in future.

I was very clever and fast enough when I was about fifteen years of age to know which was bad and good, which was to be done or not to be done. But this time I just began to experience the difficulties, hardships, punishments, etc., but I had not yet experienced the difficulties, hardships, punishments, risk, dangers, etc., of the adventures.

I noticed carefully this time that my father was a very poor old man. He was so poor that everybody in his village had strong belief that he was indeed destined with poverty. He was a farmer by profession and he was a hard working man who had farms more than the rest of the farmers in the village. But yet he was in a great sorrow always, because as he was working hard it was so his poverty was growing worse than ever.

He had two sons, my junior brother whose name was Alabi and I was the senior while his only daughter Ashabi, was the last to be born. But as the sons of a hard working man are always proved to be lazy, rascal, etc., so Alabi and I were so lazy that we never helped him in the farm. Of course, I was not interested in farming as from beginning. At last, when he became entirely old and weary and could not even work in the farm, he began to buy our food, clothes and the rest of our needs in credits. But one day, when he failed to pay some of his debts, his creditor treated him very shamefully. Having seen this treatment, I was greatly annoyed and then at the same time I invited my junior brother, Alabi, to one corner of the house. I told him thus: "My junior brother, we are old enough to go abroad to find a kind of a job to do. When we work hard for some years and save a considerable amount of money, then we shall come back and give the money to our old father and mother and by so doing they will free from their debts and poverty."

Without any argument, my junior brother agreed to my advice at the same time. In the following morning, I invited my father, mother and Ashabi, my junior sister, to the sitting-room. I told them that Alabi and I were leaving them that morning for abroad to find a job to do. He and my mother replied that they were pleased. Then I asked from my father what would he give us to take along with us. But with sorrow he replied that as we had already known he had nothing except his hoes, cutlasses, farm jumpers and aprons. So without hesitation, I put on one of his aprons and one of his farm jumpers and so my junior brother did. After that I put his two hoes and cutlasses in one basket and my junior brother carried it. Then we bade them good-bye and in return they prayed for us that we would return to them safely. It was like that we left my father's village that morning, to an unknown place.

After we had travelled so many miles, we came to the end of the path on which we had been travelling, when it was about six in the evening. Then we stopped when the darkness came. But of course, there was new moon which was not yet so bright. But as there was nothing for us to eat and we were badly hungry, therefore we were unable to sleep well till the daybreak. Very early in the morning, we woke up and with empty stomachs we continued our journey in an endless jungle. After we had travelled about two miles in that jungle without meeting anybody in it, we were very lucky to see many ripen mangoes, paw-paws and many other kinds of fruits which were scattered all over the bottom of a big tree. We believed that those fruits were brought there from a far farm by monkeys and other kinds of climbing animals. We stopped and with greediness, we ate as many as we could, and also picked better ones into our basket which we were going to eat when we were starved again.

Having rested for two hours, we continued to travel along and we travelled till the evening before we stopped and ate the rest fruits. After that we lay on a big fallen tree and slept on it till morning. But we travelled for nine days in that endless jungle before we could reach the middle of it. As both of us had already tired and weary, so we stopped under the cool shadow of a gigantic tree.

As we were resting and also discussing of what to eat, there we noticed that more than two hundred small and big birds were crying terribly and flying round an old woman. One big ostrich was in front of that old woman. The ostrich was so big and tall that we were unable to see the old woman clearly. It was walking here and there as if it was guiding the woman. If the woman walked to her left or right that ostrich would do the same thing and would spread its wings on her and all those birds were also crying terribly and rushing to wherever the old woman went.

In the first instance we thought to run away for our lives but we could not do so for we did not know where to run to in that endless jungle and instead, we were looking at her as she was wobbling towards us. When she was near us, we saw her clearly. Her body was downy but she wrapped herself from knees to the waist with the skin of a tiger and the rest parts were soft feathers. The feathers were really grown out from her body except her head which had white thick hair. Her eyes were red and hollow with old age. Her breasts were hardly to see because soft feathers were covered them. Almost all her teeth had fallen out so that made her mouth to be moving up and down always as if she was eating something in the mouth.

When she was approached us nearer and looked up suddenly and saw us, then she was coming to us direct. To our fear again immediately the curious ostrich perceived us as we were looking at them with great fear, it became very wild and then rushed furiously against us to cut us into pieces, but we hastily stood up and leaned on that gigantic tree under which we had seated all the while. And again, those small and big birds left the old woman and rushed to us. They started to cry terribly and scratch us with claws repeatedly until the old woman wobbled to that spot. Immediately she came, they parted for her to see us well and the ostrich walked to her left.

As we were still wondering and trembling with fear from feet to head, she started to ask with a fearful, huge and weak voice: "What do both of you come to do in my land or do you not know that this is my jungle?" I answered at the same time with a trembling voice: "We are sorry to come to your jungle, old woman. But I shall be glad if you will spare me a few minutes more just to explain to you of what we were finding about before we came to your jungle." Then she said as she was obstructing that ostrich several times with her left hand whenever it wanted to run against us, "Yes, I am pleased to hear your explanations, boys!" Then I started to explain to her as my junior brother, Alabi, was looking on with fear: "Yes, you see, our father and mother are so poor that they could not even feed us. For this reason, both of us were determined to go abroad and find a job to do, so that we might get money to give to them when we return to them."

This old woman paused for a while except her teethless mouth which was moving up and down without chewing anything. As she paused all of her birds perched on her shoulders and head, kept quiet and were looking at us as if they heard our grievances. Then after a while, she asked: "By the way, do you know my name?" Both of us said with one voice: "We don't know it!" Then she said: "My name is 'Jungle Witch'. I am the owner of this jungle from the beginning of the earth. Nobody live here with me except these birds (she pointed finger to them) whom I had changed from persons into birds for they had trespassed my jungle like two of you!" But immediately she mentioned her name to us, "Jungle Witch", all of her birds flew round her and then perched again on her body. So that showed us that they honoured her. They perched quietly and were listening to her as before.

We were so much feared that we nearly to fall down when she explained to us that her name was "Jungle Witch" and also when she told us that those birds were once persons before they had trespassed her jungle. My junior brother looked at my eyes with fear instead to speak out to me and in return, I looked at the ground with the same fear instead to reply him with mouth. We were in this fear when she asked again whether we knew anything about her ostrich and we said: "No!" Then she explained: "You see this ostrich" (she pointed finger to it). When we said: "Yes," she told us: "This ostrich had been a very beautiful woman before. But she had betrayed me and married to my husband after I had divorced him, then with my power, I changed her into the form of ostrich. So I started to ride her about like a horse. Her name when she was a woman was Ata. But since when I had changed her into the ostrich, she is laying two dangerous eggs every month instead born human babies. The eggs are so dangerous that all that she had laid had changed all who had trespassed my jungle and who had offended me into many forms."

When the Jungle Witch had related her story to us, we were so much wondered that we were unable to talk but we were looking at her and her birds. After a while she asked again: "Will you be able to keep my law and warning?" But when I told her that we would keep it, she said: "All right, if you can do so both of you will leave this my jungle with plenty of money and other wealths. But it is doubtful because none of those who had trespassed my jungle had returned to their towns or villages. As you have promised that you would keep my warning and law, all right, follow me now!" Immediately she had told us like that the ostrich lowered itself in her front and she mounted it and we were following her as her birds were flying round her and crying along greatly.

We did not travel more than two miles when we came to a part of that jungle which was full of cola-nut trees. She took us round the cola-nut trees first and then told us: "You are in charge of all these cola-nut trees as from today. All the cola-nuts which the trees may bear are for you. If you wish you can be carrying the nuts to the nearest market for sale. But be sure that you are keeping the money you are selling the nuts so that you can get a considerable amount of money to give to your father and mother when you return to them!" After she had told us like that, she took us to a big hut which was not so far away from the cola-nut trees. She told us to be living in it. There were several images in the front of that hut. They were in a single line and faced the hut and at the extreme left of them there was a deep pit. That pit was covered with a wooden tray. After she had shown the hut to us, she came down from her ostrich and all her birds were perched on the heads of that images. Then she walked to the images and we walked to her. As she stood before them she pointed finger to the covered pit and warned us that we must not remove the cover of it or to see what were in it or if we did so, it meant we were against her warning and therefore we would be punished for it. She explained further that, that was the warning which she had already asked from us whether we would keep it and that we had promised her that we would keep it. But she did not tell us what were inside that pit or why we should not remove the cover of it.

Then she turned to those images, and we were following her as she was inspecting them one by one. After a while she began to tell us that every one of the images was a person but with her power she had turned him into the form of image for he had trespassed her jungle. She explained furthermore that we too could change into that of images if we disobeyed her. But of course, when she told us like that I hastly interrupted that it was too risky to live in her jungle and that we would leave there for another place because we did not want to turn into images at all. But with great annoyance, she replied at the same time that willing or not, once we had come to her jungle we would not be allowed to go away without being tested or if we attempted to leave there after she had gone away we would turn into the images at once.

Now, as we heard like that from her again, another serious fear came into our minds. We did not know what to do again more than to agree to what she had told us to do. Immediately this Feather Woman or the Jungle Witch had explained to us like that, she walked back to her changeling ostrich and mounted it. She started to ride it along on a rough narrow path which was behind that hut and her birds were making great noises as they were following her. To our surprise and fear was that after a few seconds we did not see her and her birds on that path. Whether she was disappeared with her birds or sunk into the ground, we did not understand but that was another fear and embarrassment to us.

After this Feather Woman or Jungle Witch had disappeared, I went back to that images. I was looking at them with wonder. When I noticed well, I saw that they were real human beings in appearance although their bodies were mud. And when I touched their bodies were warming as if blood was in them. Sometime they seemed as if they winked and sometime as if they attempted to move the heads, arms and legs. So that showed me that in fact, they were alive although they were partly mud. Again I noticed their surroundings and I saw that there were plenty of broken and worn-out whips were lying all over the ground and in the front of them and that showed me as well that the Feather Woman used to flog them whenever she liked.

Having seen all that again, I went back to the hut, Alabi and I sat down quietly, every one of us supported his jaw with left palm and we were looking at every part of the jungle which was as quiet as a grave yard. After a while, just to expel our fear and sorrow for some time, I went around the hut, I collected some wood and brought them to the hut. I made fire in the fireplace or hearth which was in the hut. After we warmed our bodies for some minutes and we forgot our fear and sorrow then we went far away from there. We collected plenty of big fresh fruits and brought them back to the hut. Then we roasted some of them in the fire. But to our fear again, as we were eating that nuts, all that images were seemed that moment as if they were begging us to give them from the roasted nuts to eat as well.

When it was night and when the jungle had become too dark, we made big fire near the hut before we slept that night. But it was hardly in the following morning when I saw that this old woman, the Jungle Witch, rode her changeling ostrich to the hut. The noises of her birds woke Alabi, for he was still sleeping. Having noticed us that we were still in there, she rode direct to the images and when she came down from the ostrich, she put down the bunch of the strong whips which she had put on the back of the ostrich. The whips were more than one hundred. Then as both of us stood up, held the pillar of the hut, kept quiet and were looking on with great fear. There we saw that she took one of the whips, she walked to the extreme right of the images. She started to flog all of them as she was walking up and down in front of them. She flogged every one of them from head to feet until the whole whips were torn into pieces. As she was flogging them it was so she was snorting and sneezing repeatedly. And with her snappishness, so she was abusing and scorning them despite they were seemed as if they were sobbing as she was flogging them repeatedly.

She left them to flog when the whole whips were torn into pieces and then she mounted her ostrich back and rode away at the same time. But to our fear and embarrassment, those images groaned for about two hours before they could stop.

When it was about seven o'clock of that morning, after we had eaten the rest fruits, we took our cutlasses and went to the nearest palm-tree. We cut some palm-fronds and we wove many baskets from them. Then from there we went to the place of the coal-nut trees. We plucked plenty of the nuts and after they were peeled, we put them in the baskets and then carried them to the hut.

In the following morning we expected that the Jungle Witch would come to flog the images but she did not come that morning. Having waited till about nine o'clock just to see how she would flog them again but she did not come, then we carried the cola-nuts to the nearest market as she had told us to do. Of course, we wondered greatly to see such a famous market in that hidden place because such a famous market should not be near that jungle. But of course, the sort of people that we met there were quite different and together with their movements and the way of their talking to one another, were very suspicious.

But to our gladness, we sold the nuts for a considerable amount of money. Out of the money, we bought coco-yams and many kinds of food stuffs and then we came back to the hut and dug a deep pit in one corner of the hut. We put the rest money in it and then covered the pit with a flat plank. That pit was our safe. Then we were waiting for the market day which was every fifth day. And we did not attempt to see what were in that pit at all for the Feather Woman had warned us not to remove the cover of the pit which was near the images and see what were in it.

But when it was four days after the woman had come and flogged the images, she came again with another bunch of whips. She whipped them one by one until the whole whips were torn into pieces as the first time. Of course, when she was still flogging them and I saw how mercilessly she was flogging them, I did not know when I went and knelt before her and I started to beg her to pardon them. But I wondered that she was so annoyed that she spat on my eyes suddenly and then said with great anger: "Of course, both of you will soon change into the images as well!" When she told me like that, I was so afraid that I hastily left her and then entered the hut. After she had flogged and scorned them to her satisfaction, she mounted her ostrich back and rode away with her birds which were crying and following her.

After we had spent about two years in that jungle and we had saved enough money, then we were preparing with gladness to return to our village. But unfortunately, our young sister, Ashabi, whom we had left with our father and mother, had left the village this time. She was looking for us when our father and mother were anxious greatly to see us. Because both were not sure whether we had been killed by the wild animals or we had lost in the jungle. They told Ashabi that wherever she might meet us, whether we had got money or not, she must bring us back to them.

One morning, as she was wandering about, she met us in the market when we were selling the cola-nuts. But of course, we could not recognize her at first when she saluted us for we did not think that she could come to such a far, dangerous and hidden market as this one. But when she explained herself to us we did and then we embraced her with gladness. So we did not keep so long in the market on that day as we had been doing before but we returned to the jungle with her as quickly as possible.

"So my people I shall continue to tell you the remaining story of my first journey next night. I wish every one of you good luck."

Then after my people drank the remaining of their palm-wine, sang and danced for a while then they went back to their houses.

But they did not come with their musical instruments this first night.

I Was Turned into the Image for Two Years by the Witch of the Jungle

The entertainment of the second night

All the people of the village were gathered in front of my house and were served with the palm-wine. When they drank and danced and sang for a few minutes, then I continued to relate the last story of my first journey as follows:

Immediately we had returned to the hut in the jungle, after we had put the empty baskets down and put the money that we had sold the cola-nuts of that day in the usual pit. Then we cooked our food. As we were eating with our sister, Ashabi, she started to tell us the news of our father and mother and also the news of our village. She told us that our father and mother were still in their great poverty. But when she told us like that we assured her that they would be no more in poverty as soon as we returned to them because we had saved a lot of money and she was happy to hear like that from us.

Having finished with the food, we showed her that covered pit and warned her very seriously not to attempt to remove the cover of it or to see what was inside it. We explained to her furthermore that the Jungle Witch had warned us not to tamper with it. After that we showed her the images. At the first instance, she thought that they were persons but were pretended to be like that of images that moment when she stood before them. When it remained six days for us to leave for our village with all the monies that we had saved and also with several expensive dresses, etc. that we had bought. One morning, after we had carried the cola-nuts to the market,

The entertainment of the second night

As we left Ashabi in the hut, to prepare our food. But soon after we had left for the market, the Jungle Witch rose her usual changeling ostrich to the hut. Then she started to flog the images as usual, but as that was the first time that Ashabi saw her there. She was so much feared that she left the hut and came to us in the market. Having told us about her with throbbing heart, we did not waste time but we returned to the hut with her at the same time but the old woman had gone away. Anyhow, we prepared our food and after had eaten it. Then we stood up and walked to the images just to see how they had been flogged that morning by the woman.

But as my junior brother, Alabi, Ashabi and I were looking at the images and were praying to God to change them back to their former forms, we did not notice when Ashabi left us and went to that covered pit. She said loudly: "By the way, what kinds of things are in this pit which are forbidden to a person to see!" And without hesitation, she removed the cover of it. When she saw two ostrich eggs in it, she took them out. But when we saw her did so, we hardly shouted greatly: "Ah! put the eggs back into the pit!" when Alabi and I were changed into the images unexpectedly. We were at the extreme right in the same line with the other images.

Ashabi did not believe her eyes at first when she did not see us any more but the two new images. When she looked around the hut and yet did not see us but her alone, she was so puzzled that she became mad at the same time. After a while, she ran to us, she held us and was shaking us with all her power and so she was calling our names loudly perhaps we might change back to our own forms, but nevertheless, we did not change at all. Having tried all her efforts but all were in vain, then she stood before us, she was weeping continuously and was blaming herself that if she had known she would not have removed the cover of the pit or to take the two eggs out of the pit.

The entertainment of the second night

After a while, the darkness of the night came, every part of the hut and the jungle was very dark. Now Ashabi remained alone in the darkness, there was nobody with her and that was another fear to her. Having wept bitterly for some hours before us then she walked back to the hut, she sat and continued to weep sorrowfully in the darkness.

But to our surprise, as we had already turned into the form of images, we were feeling whenever something touched us. We were hearing whenever somebody talked but when we talked people did not hear us. We were breathing in and out but people could not see our breasts to move and we could see everything and think as when we had not changed into the images.

Hardly in the following morning, when the Jungle Witch rode her usual ostrich to the hut. When she came down from it, she put one bunch of whips down before us (images). After her birds were perched on our heads and shoulders, she walked into the hut and met Ashabi in the corner as she was weeping bitterly. Then without mercy, she asked from her: "Where are your two brothers? Where are they? Have they caught by my trap?" But Ashabi, with tears rolling down her cheeks, pointed finger to us and said: "Look, old mother, my two brothers had changed into the images last night!" Then the Jungle Witch turned her fearful eyes to us and hastily interrupted without mercy: "Oh, very good! I am very lucky indeed that my images are increased by two! Very good! I know, they could not keep my warnings!" Having said like that with gladness and great laughter and Ashabi was looking at her with expectancy that she would change us back to our former forms, she left her (Ashabi) in the hut and wobbled to us. She dragged the bunch of the whips nearer.

When she took one whip and then stood before us, before she started to flog us she said: "Yes, I had known that one day would be one day when both of you would be caught by my trap and you have already caught by it!" Then without mercy, she started to flog us one by one. Whenever one whip was worn out she would take another one and then continued. Thus she flogged us until the whole bunch of the whips were torn into pieces.

When Ashabi saw how mercilessly she was flogging us, she came to her, she knelt before her and with tears she started to beg her to change us back our own forms. But the cruel Jungle Witch hastily said: "Not at all! No pardon in my jungle! I have never pardoned any offender in my life, it is a thing that I hate most to do. You, as the pleader will soon be turned into an ostrich and I will be riding you about because this present one (she pointed finger to that ostrich) is getting old and weary!"

After she had explained to Ashabi like that she mounted her ostrich back and was singing loudly as she was riding it along on her usual narrow path which went deeply into the jungle and all her birds were following her as well. We wept for severe pains when she was flogging us, we attempted to run away for our lives but we could not move to a bit. After she had gone away then Ashabi returned to the hut. She cast down with sorrow and was looking at us several times in one moment perhaps we would change back to our former forms but all her hope was in vain.

Within a few days that we had changed into the images and that the Feather Woman or Jungle Witch had started to flog us severely every morning, Ashabi was so leaned that bones were appeared on every part of her body. She was always lonely and casting down in the corner of the hut. But as the Jungle Witch had said before she had left that morning that she would change Ashabi into the form of ostrich when she came back to flog us in the following morning. So Ashabi, feared of that, attempted to leave us and escape to our village, but of course, after she had travelled a short distance away from the hut, she came back and sat down in the hut as usual when she remembered us. She was unable to leave us.

She hardly sat in the corner when one old man entered the hut when it was about one o'clock of that night. That old man was entirely bent down with old age. He was walking with a long and thick stick. The stick was sparkling as if it was polishing every moment. Immediately he entered the hut, he crawled to one long stool which was before the hearth. He leaned his walking-stick on the floor nearly to touch the hearth. But with great fear, Ashabi hastily stopped weeping immediately she saw the old man crawling towards to the hearth. After he had seated well on the stool, he started to gather pieces of sticks into the hearth. Having done that, he put big firewood on those dried sticks, after that he took two small stones from his native cap which was on his head. He held each of the stones in each hand and then he started to strike one from the other until several hot sparks of the stones ignited the dried pieces of the sticks and after a while it became a big fire and a few minutes more, the fire became a big flame and shone to every part of the hut and then he started to warm his body. I was seeing him as he was doing all these things although we were in form of images.

Through the flame we saw him clearly that he had one leg only, the other one had been cut off from a long time. As he was snivelled it was so he was sneezing and snorting continuously. As he was still doing like that, the wooden pillar on which he leaned, as he was enjoying the heat of the fire, broke and again the four legs of the stool on which he sat broke and then he was falling along on to the hearth. But that was a great funny to us, because as he was just trying to safe himself from the fire, a large soot fell on his head from the dirty ceiling and it caught fire unexpectedly. But as he stood up suddenly, forgetting that he had one leg only, and the fire was burning his head so painfully that he did not remember to take his walking-stick to support himself, and as he was shouting loudly for help, he staggered to the corner in which Ashabi cast down and then he fell on her suddenly without knowing that anybody was there. He was so feared that he staggered to another corner and fell down again when he heard the voice of Ashabi unexpectedly.

As he was doing like that, we did not know when we bursted into a great laughter but nobody could hear us. We had forgotten all our pains and sorrow that moment. And Ashabi who had been hiding herself from him all the while, did not know when she too bursted into a great laughter like us for she had forgotten her sorrow that moment. And it was that midnight I had discovered that "amusement" was the father of "sorrow". Because Ashabi who had already leaned to the bones, regained her strength at the same time when she had seen the amusements which that old man had presented and we, as the images, had forgotten our morning punishment which the Jungle Witch was giving us.

After Ashabi had pulled out herself from him, then she helped him to stand and then took him back to the hearth. She gave him another stool and repaired the fire as well. After that she sat a little distance from him. But as he was puzzled that moment, so it was after he had warmed himself and rested for a while before he was able to thank Ashabi for helping him.

But to his surprise and fear, he hardly thanked Ashabi when she continued to weep. Then with lower voice he asked from her: "Lady, what are you weeping for?" Ashabi replied that: "I am weeping for my two brothers (she pointed to us and the old man gazed at us (images) with wonder). And I had tried all my efforts to change them back to their own forms but all my efforts had failed and I must not return to my father and mother without them."

When she had explained to the old man, he shook head with

pity and then explained to her: "Your brothers were very lucky that you were with them before they were changed into the images otherwise they would remain like that for ever. But you will safe your brothers if you can endure the pain. The pain is that you will pretend to be dump for the period of two years. But if you talk a single word or you simply make "ah" within that years or before that period expire, your brothers will certainly remain as images for ever. To be dump for two years is the only medicine which can change your brothers back to their former forms. You see, if the rest images had sisters or anybody else like your brothers, who can pretend to be dump for that period, they will not remain as images for ever. And furthermore, as far as I have seen, one beautiful man will come to this hut before morning. When he comes and talks to you, please do not reply, but just pretend to be dump. I thank you very much for helping me to stand up when I had fallen on you. So I am going away now." Then the old man supported himself to stand up with his sparkling walking-stick and he walked zigzag out of the hut and after a while he disappeared into the darkness as Ashabi was still following him along with eyes.

Although we were images but we heard all what the old man had told Ashabi to do which could change us back to our own forms. I attempted to speak to him to change us back at the same time or before long but he did not hear my voice. But as the old man had told Ashabi, to our surprise, it was not so long from when he had disappeared into the darkness when a heavy rain came. Within a few minutes that the rain had started, a beautiful young man with a gun and hunting-bag on shoulder, rode a beautiful horse to the hut. When he came down from the horse, he fastened the rope of his horse on me, for he thought I was an ordinary image. The rope was fastened on my waist so hardly that I was hardly breathing in and out.

Then he entered the hut with the hope to shelter himself

from the heavy rain. But he was greatly surprised and shocked when he saw Ashabi before the fire. At the first instance, he did not believe his eyes but he thought that she was a jungle spirit who came to warm herself with the fire. So to make sure whether she was a jungle spirit or a real person, he hastily took one juju-gourd from his left elbow. The juju-gourd was fastened on his elbow with the vein of antelope. He removed its cock and poured some juju-powder from it on that fire. Then he cocked the gourd back and fastened it back on his left elbow. But when the powder started to burn and smell and Ashabi did not run away or disappear, then he was quite sure that she was a real person. So he put more dried stocks in the fire which made it to bring out new powerful flames and it shone to every part of the hut. Now, through the flames he saw her that she was a very beautiful lady but he was puzzled how she came to such a terrible jungle as that one.

This hunter was the prince of a big town which was about ten miles away from that jungle. He was hunting about in that dead night when he accidentally entered this jungle, but when the rain came, he was finding shelter about until when he came to that hut. When he stared at her very well and saw that she was a very beautiful lady, he asked with wonder: "Ah, what are you doing here, you a very beautiful lady like this?" but Ashabi did not reply, she pretended to be dump.

"What is your name? From which village did you come to this hut which belongs to the Witch of the Jungle?" the prince caressed and asked her again, but Ashabi did not reply at all, she was simply looking on as if she was a real dump lady. "Are you dump?" the prince paused for a while probably she would reply this time but Ashabi would not. "If you are a dump lady or not, I will take you to my town to be my wife!" When the beauty of Ashabi attracted the prince, he simply helped her to stand up (the rain had stopped then). He took her to his horse and put her on it and after that he started to loose the rope of the horse away from my waist. But as he was doing so, Ashabi, with tears rolling down her cheeks, was giving sign to the hunter or prince that I was her brother but had changed into the image through her fault but the prince did not understand the sign she made.

As the prince was taking her to his town which we did not know, she was looking at her back just to see us whether we would change back to our own forms that time but it was in vain. As we were in form of images, I was telling the prince repeatedly to tell me the name of his town so that I might know where Ashabi was but he did not pay heed to all what I told him because he did not hear my voice. It was like that Ashabi was taken away by an unknown man to an unknown town. She could not refuse to go and could not tell the prince not to tie the rope of his horse on my waist because she must not talk for two years and that meant we would remain in form of images for two years before we would be able to change back to our former forms or if Ashabi was mistakenly talked it meant we would remain as images for ever and that was another fear and sorrow to us. The horse had kicked me, bit me, snorted on my body which was mud and scratched my head with its snout but I could not move my hands to defend myself.

When the hunting prince brought Ashabi to his town and showed her to his royal family, they were very happy but they were very sad at last when they discovered that she was dump. Because it was against the law of their town for a prince to marry a dump lady. The reason was that the people of that town did not like the son of a dump woman to become their king in the future. Therefore, the kingmakers and the royal family advised the prince not to marry Ashabi and to return her to where he had brought her at once. But he rejected their advice entirely.

At last, the royal family and the kingmakers gathered together, they made a secret meeting that whenever Ashabi gave birth to a baby, they would kill the baby on the very day it was named. Although the prince was not present when they had plotted to do so but Ashabi was present and she heard what they were going to do to her baby, but of course, she must not talk otherwise both of us would remain as images for ever. The royal family and the kingmakers did not hide that secret plot from Ashabi for they believed she was real dump and by that she would not be able to hear words. It was a great sorrow to her to hear what would be done to her baby, but she was still pretending to be a dump lady.

After a few months, Ashabi gave birth to a male baby and according to the royal family's and the kingmakers' plot. The beautiful baby was killed after a few minutes that a name was given to it. It was killed on the present of Ashabi and she was about to talk to them that she was not dump so that her baby might be spared. But it came to her mind that moment that if she talked, both of us would remain as images for ever. And each time she gave birth to a baby, thus it was killed without mercy on the naming day by the kingmakers. But when she gave birth to the third baby, her Creator was so good that it was on the very day that her baby would be named and then be killed like others, the two years that she must not talk expired. Her baby was hardly named when it was lay down and as the killer was just taking his knife nearly to touch its neck. Then the moment that Ashabi was at liberty to talk was reached. So she hastily held the hand of the killer and then she talked loudly: "Please, don't kill my baby! I was not dump as all of you had thought!" But the people were very surprised when she talked and then her baby was spared at once.

After that she explained to them why she had pretended to be dump for two years. And when she told them about her brothers who had changed into the images since two years ago by the Jungle Witch, the people accompanied her to the jungle. But to her surprise, we had changed back to our own forms before she arrived with the people, but the rest images were still there. With gladness and shout of joy, Ashabi ran to us and embraced us when she met us in the form of persons and all those people wished us good luck after they had looked at us with wonder for a few minutes.

As we were dancing, singing loudly with great joy and telling those people about the Jungle Witch that after Ashabi had been taken away by the hunting prince, she (Jungle Witch) had been giving us double punishment when she did not see Ashabi in the hut any more. We were still telling them the story when she rode her usual ostrich to the hut but after she had put the bunch of whips down, she saw many people in her hut. She hesitated and scowled at us for a few minutes before she walked nearer and then asked: "Who are you? What do you want in my hut? Oh, I am very happy, I shall have more images today!"

But when none of us paid heed to all of her questions, but we were still enjoying our new lives with the people. Then with great anger, she was walking along to that pit in which there were two ostrich eggs, to expose them to us so that the whole of us might be changed into the images. Having understood what she wanted to do, Ashabi hastily took one of the firewood from the hearth, she went to the pit. After she had closed her eyes well, she removed the cover of it and then broke them before the Jungle Witch wobbled to the pit. But to our surprise, immediately the eggs exploded loudly, the rest images and that ostrich changed into persons suddenly and the Jungle Witch herself fell down and fainted at the same time. It was that time it revealed to us that the rest images, the ostrich and also those birds which were following her about, were persons like ourselves and it was that time it had just revealed to us that if the two eggs were broken, all the images, etc. would change back to their proper forms, otherwise Ashabi should had broken them the very day that we had become images. Great noises arose as soon as they had changed into persons. They were thanking the Creator and were shouting with great joy as we had done.

Some of them were women of about forty years of age and some were young ladies, boys and middle-aged men. They told us that they had changed into the images when they had removed the cover of the pit and seen the two ostrich eggs which were inside it. Then I entered the room of the hut, I took the money which we had saved in selling the cola-nuts but all the dresses had been damaged by the insects. So the whole of us left the hut and were singing and dancing along on the road to the town of the hunting prince.

When we got to that town, we were taken to the king direct by that people. Luckily when we related the story of our father and mother to the king, the father of the hunting prince, he gave us many presents and money. After we had lived with him for about one month, we returned to our village, but some of the rest people who had been changed into persons like ourselves, stayed with the king because they could not trace out their respective towns and villages.

My father and mother and the people of the village were very sorry when they heard what had happened to us. Out of the money that we brought to them, they paid all their debts and bought all their needs as well.

Now my people, I will repeat it before you this night, that I will not forget the Jungle Witch or the Feather Woman of the jungle throughout my life time. I believe, every one of you had heard the hardship, punishment, etc. of my first journey? Then the people roared at a time: "It was a terrible journey indeed although you had returned with money!"

"I thank you very much for listening to the story of my

past adventures and I shall start to tell you another entertainment of my second journey, tomorrow night, good night to every one of you!" Then my people sang and danced for a few minutes before they went back to their houses, because they brought their drums and many other musical instruments this night.

The Treacherous Queen and the King in the Bush of Quietness

The entertainment of the third night

My second Journey

It was hardly nine o'clock of the third night when the people of my village came to my house to enjoy the entertainment of my second adventure. All sat as usual and everyone was served with one keg of palm-wine. But this third night, they brought with them some drums, horns and many other of the native musical instruments, because we were badly disappointed about the musical instruments the first night. Then I sat on my usual old armchair in front of them. As the moon was shining and the cool breeze of that dry season was blowing very quietly. Then after everyone had drunken of his or her palm-wine and I put fire in my smoking pipe. I first addressed the people: "You see, my people, my motto this night is that this world is not equal. So all my adventures were not the same. One who has head has no money to buy hat and one who has money to buy hat has no head on which to put it. But my people, please put it in your minds as from this night that under this sun, there is nobody who is above temptation. So this night, I am going to tell you about a treacherous queen who had not pleased with all money that her husband, the king, had been giving to her. Please listen well."

Then with one voice my people shouted that they are listening to me. So after they drank some palm-wine and then sang and danced for a while, I started to relate the story of my second adventure as follows:

The entertainment of the third night

After a few months that I had returned from my first journey in which I had been changed into an image for the period of two years. I thought over one midnight that although, I had met much difficulties, etc., in my first journey, but yet, I had not experienced it as much as of those old people. Because if an old man tells all his difficulties, hardships, losses, etc., which he had met before he becomes old. Many young men would prefer to die while young just to avoid these things. Therefore, if I gave up my adventures this time, it would be shameful to me. So for that reason, in the following morning, I invited almost all the people of the village to my father's house. After the drinks were served, then I announced loudly that I would start my second journey the following morning. So all the old men among the people praised me greatly for my bravery and after that the whole gathering wished me good luck before they went back to their houses after many songs were sung and drums were beaten.

In the following morning, I took one gun, hunting-bag, matchet and some yams and then I bade my father and mother good-bye before I left the village. But my junior brother, Alabi, did not follow me this time. I told him to stay at home to be taking care of them. I travelled more than two weeks before I reached a town. That town was not so big but almost all the inhabitants were rich, so this made me to stop my journey there.

When I was escorted to the king, I explained to him that I was finding wealths about. But he laughed at me first before he said that I would get what I wanted from him provided I could help him to find out his lost prince for him. But I asked with wonder whether his prince had been kidnapped, disappeared or lost. He explained to me that he could not say what had happened to him because one morning, when he went to the town in which his prince lived, there was nothing found, there were no houses and people as before, all had been disappeared, but there was a fearful quiet bush instead. That king explained to me further that since that time, he heard nothing about his prince or the people of that town.

Having told me the story of his prince, the food and drink were brought and I dined and drank together with him. In the following morning, I took my gun, hunting-bag and my matchet and then I told the king to take me to the spot of the disappeared town. Without a word, he followed me and we travelled more than ten miles before we reached the spot of the disappeared town at about one o'clock p.m. When he showed the spot to me, he returned to his town at the same time and then it remained I alone in that quiet bush.

Having travelled far away in it, I stopped, I made the fire near a tree, I roasted some yams and ate them. After that I stood up and continued to roam about, just to find out what had happened to the prince, etc. But after a while, I stopped near a big tree just to listen to the cries of the doves because I liked to know the time or the hour of the day. But of course, there was no any voice of a bird or any living creature was heard. In that quiet bush, there was no single living creature, even there were no ants or flies and again, to my fear, all of the trees were stood still as if there was no breeze or air. Everything was very quiet in a terrible way so that I was always shocked with fear every moment.

Anyhow, I was still travelling deeply into this bush of quietness until when the darkness disallowed me to see. Then when I could not see, I stopped, I lay down as I was thinking about the disappearance of the prince and his wife, etc. It was not so long when I fell asleep when I began to dream. And it was not so long when I was dreaming when I saw that I was in a big town. I saw many people and the prince that they were in a great severe punishment. Some could not walk while some were walking about in that disappeared town but with much difficulties. Having seen them in my dream like that, I was so feared that I attempted to go away from that bush so that I might not be one of them. But as I attempted to go away, one of the people held my arm and then he was dragging me back.

As I was trying to take my arm back from him and I was unable to do so, I shouted with fear: "Leave my arm and let me go away from this town!" But as I shouted with fear, I woke and that time was about twelve o'clock in the night. Then I stood up and rubbed my eyes with palm. But hardly walked to a short distance from that spot when I began to hear that a person was bitterly groaning from a long distance.

Without fear, I started to find the person who was groaning like that about in the darkness. And I did not go far when I was seeing a big house in front. When I went nearer to it, I saw that a dim ray of light was penetrated to the outside through one of the windows. Then I went to that window with fear, I peeped in but I could not see anything in that house except the bitter groan of a person which was hearing. Again, I held my gun ready on my shoulder while I held the matchet ready with the right hand, then I walked cautiously to the main gate of the house which had no door and I peeped in as I dangled my right foot on that entrance. But yet, I did not see anything in there except the flame of a native mud lamp which I saw far away in one of the rooms at the extreme left. That lamp was dimly burning with the palm-oil.

As I still dangled my right foot on the door, I noticed that the main gate had a portico which resembled that of an ancient palace of the olden days king. Several images like that of the lions, tigers, deers, antelopes, monkeys, crocodiles, lizards, men, women, etc. were carved on that portico from bottom to top. But some parts of them had been washed away by the rains and all together with the portico were very old. In the veranda, there were several sprouts of the small trees. The frames, roof, ceiling, etc. were nearly eaten off by the white ants. Chairs, stools, benches, mats and tables were so old that they had fallen and scattered all over the veranda. Several insect moulds were seen everywhere. Again I noticed that this house had a very big and square premises which resembled that of the premises of the ancient palace. There were many shrines of the god of smallpox, god of thunder, god of iron, god of river, etc. which had been worshipped from a long time. So all these things showed me that this house was the palace of a powerful king before. But what had happened to the king who had been living in there, I could not say yet.

But as the groan of a person was still hearing more terribly from the extreme right of the house, so I entered and I was walking very cautiously along on the veranda to the extreme right. It was so I was walking along with great fear until when I came to a large room. Then I stopped and peeped in and to my surprise and fear, I saw one man who lay on the floor. One big mud lamp which was burning with the palm-oil was in a little distance in front of him, one old chair which had been damaged by the insects was in the right corner of that room. One of its four legs had been broken off and this made it to lean against that corner.

But to my surprise, that man did not see me when I entered the room, stood before him and I was listening to his groan. Of course, with fear, I noticed that he had been a very beautiful man before. He was about forty-five years old, his beard and moustache had over-grown and were touching his breast so these showed me that he was lay down there from a long time. His body was full of sores which were caused by whip and pieces and splits of whip were lying all over that room.

As he was groaning loudly and continuously as if he was put in the fire and as his pains were so much that he could not see me. So I walked cautiously nearer to him, I leaned my gun on my waist, I hung my matchet back to my shoulder and then I clapped hands very quietly. He was first startled with fear as if I were the person who was giving him the pains, then he lifted up head very slightly as if it was tied to the floor and then he hesitated to hear what I came in to tell him. But as fear and wonder did not allow me to say one word that moment, so he rested his head back on the usual place and continued to groan as loudly as before. My hope was that he would sit up or stand up if he heard my claps, but he could not do neither of these things.

Having listened again for a while, with a quiet voice, I asked: "Hello! How? But what is happening to you, which is so much painful that you are groaning repeatedly as if you are in the fire?" Then he tried all his best and lifted up his head a bit, he breathed out heavily with grief and with a harsh and sorrowful voice, he replied: "Yes, you are quite right to ask such a question from me. But if you know my grievances you would not be surprised to hear my groan." But when I heard his voice which showed me that he would be able to explain his grievances to me, and that he was willing to, I walked to the corner, I leaned my gun, after that I dragged that old chair, which had three legs, before him. But as I was sitting on it, I fell down and the chair itself fell apart, because I had forgotten that its fourth leg had been broken off. Therefore I stood up, I supported it with that leg and then I could sit on well.

Again, I asked quietly: "Please, tell me all your grievances probably I may be able to help you." And then after he had breathed out heavily with grief and hesitated for a while, he started to relate his story to me: "I was the king of this palace (the house in which I met him) and my father is a powerful and kind king in his town which is about ten miles away from here. During the time that I was the king of this town (the quiet bush in which that house was), I married one wife. She is very beautiful and in respect of this, I loved her so wholeheartedly that I told her every one of my secrets. Not knowing she is a powerful treacherous woman who has also supernatural power.

"But as she had noticed that I preferred to drink the drinks such as palm-wine, guinea corn-wine, bamboo-wine, etc. every night, before I slept. So not knowing that my wife had one kind of a powerful juju which she used to put in the drinks before she was bringing it to me to drink. That juju was to make me to sleep and not to wake till when the cocks crowed in the morning or I would not be able to wake from the sleep for several days if cocks were failed to crow. Alas, I did not know or outwit this beautiful clever wife that she was mixing up my drinks with juju before bringing it to me and she did so for many years successfully.

"But one midnight, as I sat in my beautiful armchair to rest for a few minutes, and as I kept very quietly as if I was sleeping. Then my attendants who thought that I had slept and as they noticed that my wife had gone to somewhere in the town, started to lament. One said to the others: 'It is a pity indeed, that our master (king) does not suspect his wife yet, that she is mixing up his drinks every night with a powerful juju!' The second lamented: 'I wonder! But the juju powder is so powerful that when our master drinks it will fall asleep at the same time and will not be able to wake by himself if cooks do not crow in the morning!' Then the third lamented: 'Very wonderful! I had noticed too that immediately our master had slept last night, the woman went out but she returned as soon as the cocks had started to crow!' And the fourth asked from the rest: 'By the way, what is she going out to do every midnight?' The rest suggested: 'Perhaps, she is going out to sleep with another man!'

"Again, the first attendant asked: 'If she is going to sleep with another man. Is that man richer than our master, the king? And that means that man is giving her more money than the king!' The fifth said angrily: 'An ordinary man can never give her enough money like our master. But of course, women are never satisfied. . . .' And the fourth suggested: 'Is it possible to tell our master the secret of his wife?' But the rest shook heads and said: 'No!' Here my attendants stopped when my wife entered.

"Thus my attendants had lamented about me without knowing that I did not sleep but I had put all they had said about my wife in mind. In the night, when I was ready to go to bed, she brought my drinks as usual. But as soon as she had left the room I threw it away and then I pretended as if I had drunken it. After that I lay on my bed and pretended as well as if I had slept. After a while she came back, she examined the tumblers just to make sure whether I had drunken it. When she saw that all the tumblers were empty, she quenched the light of the room and then she lay on the bed with me. And it was not so long when I had pretended to be asleep when she stood up. She walked to her cupboard, she opened it and took out the best of her dresses such as gold beads, rings, headgear, clothes, etc. Then she dressed up as if she was going to marry that night and after that she took out one covered calabash from the cupboard.

"When she removed the cover of it, I saw that one white creature like a small bird flew out and perched on top of that cupboard. After she had put the calabash back in the cupboard and closed it back. She held the bird with right hand above head, she faced my bed and then started to say wisperly: 'Let not this foolish and hopeless man, who calls himself the king of this town, wake till when the cocks start to crow when I shall return.'

"After that she opened one of the windows and said to the bird again: 'Let you fly out now and be driving away all the dangers and evils of the road before I come.' Having commanded it like that, she released it and then it flew away.

After that she walked to the door of the room, opened it and walked out to the sitting-room. Again she opened the door of the sitting-room which led to the main door. When she opened it and walked to the outside and I heard when she slammed it heavily, I stood up, I hastily dressed up in my big black garment. I put on my native trousers and black cap. Then I took my sword from the rack near my bed. I hung it on the shoulder and spread the garment over it, then I followed her.

"It was so she was going alone as quickly as she could in the rays of the moon and I was following her just to know where she was going that midnight. Having travelled far away, she came to the market which was at the outskirt. In the centre of the market, I saw one well-dressed man who stood in the rays of the moon and was waiting for her. Then she went to that man and she embraced him. But the man snatched himself from her and he grumbled: 'It should have been better if you have told me that you would not be able to come in time!' But as I hid myself in the dark stall which was near them, I saw my wife when she held that man again, knelt before him and started to beg him: 'Oh, my lover, don't be annoyed with me, because it was not my fault for keeping late behind. But I had been waiting for that foolish man (myself) who called himself my husband, to sleep and he had not slept in time! Therefore, don't be annoyed with me, my lover!' and she kissed the man.

"As both were doing like that, my wife began to tell all my secrets to that man. Having left that, both started to abuse me so much that they bursted into a great laughter at a time as they embraced themselves. Having seen them like that and heard all they said about me, I became so annoyed that I took my sword out of its sheath. I rushed against them and I cut the man on the waist suddenly. As he was falling down my wife escaped for her life at once. Then without hesitation, I went back to my palace through shorter road. I entered my room, after I had hung my sword back on the rack, I lay on my bed and pretended at the same time as if I had slept.

"After a while my wife entered the room. After she had shut the door gently, she loosened her dresses and put them back in her cupboard. Having waited near the window for a while, her bird flew in and perched on top of the cupboard. But to my surprise, she hardly touched it when it changed into a white round stone. Then she put that stone into that white calabash, she covered it with its lid and then put it back in the cupboard. Having done that, she walked to my bed and then lay on it. But she did not suspect at all that I was the one who had killed that man, her lover.

"As I lay on the bed, I was unable to sleep at all, but I was wondering about the evil deeds of the women till the morning. In the morning, as I was the king of this town (the quiet bush) who had the right to give an order at any time. So, I ordered my bellringer to announce round the town that all the dead bodies of the men who had died last night should be brought to my palace for examination. I did that so that my wife might know that I had seen all she had done last night. And before nine o'clock in the morning, about six dead bodies were brought to my palace and my wife's lover was among.

"But when she saw him in pool of blood, she started to weep, she could not hesitate in one place but was entering the room and coming back to look at him several times in a moment. She was greatly perplexed that time. Sometime she was driving the flies away from that dead man but she was not doing so for the rest dead bodies. After a while she brought one of her finest cover clothes and covered the man with it so that the flies might not be able to perch on him again.

"When she did so to that man only and left the rest untouched, I asked her: 'Is that dead man your relative?' But she replied with tears: 'Not at all.' I asked again: 'But you are interested in him more than the rest. Why?' She explained: 'Of course, he was a man that I knew before he had died.' I asked: 'From where did you know him, in the market place or where?' So this time she shrunk suspiciously and then she replied: 'Don't try to know about that.' When she said so, I went to my room and came out with my sword. I showed it to her. Then I explained to her that the man was her lover whom she had met in the market last midnight. I stretched the sword forward, I told her to look at it. But as she was still looking at it, I told her plainly that I had killed her lover with it last midnight and it was that time she knew that I was the man who had killed her lover.

"So immediately I had revealed her secret, she went to her cupboard and after a while she returned to me. As she stood before me sobbing continuously, she spat on my face and then said loudly: 'I command you to remain in one place until when my lover comes alive again!' But to my fear, she hardly spat on my face and commanded like that when I had lay down in this room (in the room I met him). So since the day that I had lay down in here, I could not stand up and again all the houses and the peoples in them had turned into the bush in which my palace (the house in which I met him) is. Now, it is too late before I had understood that 'the beauty of the beautiful woman is a danger'."

When this king had told me his story and then he continued to groan loudly as before, I raised my head up with wonder for a few minutes. After a while I dragged the seat nearer to him. But when I lifted the big cover cloth which was on his body, I was greatly surprised and feared to see that he was turned into a snake from feet to the waist. That part was about four feet diameter with sharp scales but it was tapered to the end (feet) like that of a tail of a big snake.

It had several kinds of colours like that of cobra. To my fear again, that part was also chained tightly and that chain went into the ground, so he was unable to move or shake at all. And from his waist to forehead was that of man but it was full of sores caused by whips.

When I first lifted up the cloth of his body and saw his half-body which had changed into that of a snake, I was so much feared that I first ran to a short distance and then shouted greatly: "Hah, a beautiful woman is a danger indeed!" Then with embarrassment, I walked back to him and I sat on the same chair and I was looking at him without knowing what to say again. After a while, when my fear had left me, I asked from him: "Please, tell me, what are you groaning for?" He stopped groaning and explained: "I am groaning for two reasons. Firstly, the part of my body which is turned into that of a snake is paining and aching me very severely, because my wife is beating it with a heavy cudgel every midnight, and secondly, I am groaning for my life which is spared for this severe punishment. I prefer to die at once than to remain like this. I am begging my Creator to take my life before this time but there is no answer."

But as he had mentioned that his wife was still coming to beat him every midnight, I asked from him where was she living. He told me that he did not know where she was coming from. Then I asked again whether she was bringing food to him whenever she came to beat him. He replied: "Not at all." I asked again: "If she does not, but what are you eating as you cannot even shake yourself how much more to stand up and walk about?" He replied: "I do not eat and I do not feel to eat since when she had changed me into this form." Furthermore, I asked: "When she stops beating you what does she do next?" He replied: "When she stops beating me she will go to the dead body of her lover which she had lay in uncovered grave in the room which is next to the end of this palace. She dug a grave in that room and lay the dead body of her lover in it since the very day she had changed me into this form." Having heard like that from this man who was the king of that palace, I stood up at the same time. I walked to the extreme end of the palace. And I saw the dead body of his wife's lover in a room over there, but it had become skeleton.

It was inside the grave which was not covered and was decorated as when a dead body was "in state". Every part of that room was very clean and was beautifully decorated by the woman. She put one big native mud lamp before the grave and it shone dimly over the grave but it needed more oil to make it brighter.

Having seen this again, I started to go from one room to another and then to the premises. As the man had told me that he was the king and that house was his palace. So when I went round the house, it showed that it was a beautiful palace before. Because everything that I saw in it were belonged to only a king, but all were very old and were nearly eaten off by the insects. The premises was full of gods and idols of all kinds but they had fallen and scattered all over the ground. Then I went back to him in the room. When I sat on the usual seat, he stopped groaning. He lifted his head up and asked me: "Did you see the dead body of my wife's lover?" I replied that I had seen it but it had become a skeleton.

Now, I told him that I would help him. But he asked with wonder how could I help him. But I told him to wait and see what I was going to do.

Then I took my gun and matchet, I went to the room in which the skeleton was. I took one cover cloth from the wall, as many fine clothes were hung all over the walls of that room by that woman. Then I went inside that grave, I lay on the skeleton, I put my gun on the left and matchet and one strong rope on the right, after that, I covered the whole of my body with that cloth. Then I was waiting for the woman to come.

When it was three o'clock in the morning, this woman entered the palace through the door of the premises. She held one mud lamp with left hand and one heavy cudgel with right hand. First, she went direct to the room in which her husband, the king, was. She beat him without mercy for about one hour. He begged her with sorrowful voice, but she did not listen to his plea. He sobbed, groaned, cried, wept and shouted for mercy but she did not stop to beat him. As she was beating him, it was so she was repeating: "You killed my lover! You killed my lover! You killed my lover!"

When she left him to beat, then she was coming with the lamp and cudgel to the room in which the skeleton of her lover was lay. But as she was coming, I saw her clearly that, she was indeed, a very beautiful woman. She was not too tall and not too short. She was not too black and not yellow and she was dressed in clothes that showed she was mourning the death of her lover. My aim was to shoot her to death immediately, but her beauty prevented me to do so and again, if I did so, her husband would not be able to change back to his former form again.

When she entered the room, she first repaired the lamp, she took one bottle of palm-oil from the corner of the room, she poured some oil from it into the lamp. When it shone to the grave and every part of the room, then she stood before the grave. First, she knelt down and she saluted the skeleton as if it was still alive. After that she stood up and said loudly: "My lover! My lover! My lover! When are you coming back to me? Have you forgotten me? Don't forget me! I am expecting you soon! For in respect of you, I had changed my husband, the king of a big town, into the form of a half-snake and I am beating him every midnight! Come! come! come back to me, my lover!" Having said like that, she wept bitterly. But when she was preparing to go out, I said loudly with a huge voice:

"Hah, my lover! My lover! My lover! I have come from the town of deads this midnight. But I will be allowed only to stay with you if you change your husband the king, back to his former form! Better you go and change him back now and then come back to help me out of this grave!"

But when she heard like that, she was so happy that she ran to her husband. She thought that I was her lover and that in fact I just woke from the dead. When she stood before her husband, I heard when she commanded very loudly: "Now, as my lover has come back to me, so I command you to change back to your former form!" She said so with a joyful voice. Her husband hardly changed when she ran back to the grave. When she came back, she stood before the grave, she stretched both hands towards me and then said: "Yes, my lover, I have done what you asked me to do. I have changed him back to his own form. Hah, welcome, my lover! I am ready now to help you out of the grave!"

Then I told her to come nearer so that my hands could reach her own. But when she came nearer and was stretching hands to hold me, I hastily snatched her own hands instead. Without hesitation, I tied both up with that rope and then I was dragging her towards the grave. But when she saw the rope in her hands and that I was pulling her towards the grave instead to come out to her, she was greatly feared. She struggled to run away, but I did not allow her to do so. She tried to cut off the rope and run away for her life but I was pulling her into the grave. After a while, she was despaired and said: "Are you not my lover?" I replied with a fearful voice: "I am not your lover at all but I am a man who come to take you to heaven now! Come inside the grave and let us go together!" But she replied with fear: "Not at all! Please leave my hands and let me go away!"

As she was still shouting with fear and struggling very roughly to escape, I jumped out of the grave. I rushed against her and held her both arms to her back so suddenly that she was nearly to faint for fear. Then I tied the rope to her both wrists. After that I left her there because she had no power again that time. I went to her husband and I met him on that old three-legged chair, on which I sat before. When I met him, he was still perplexed, he was doing like a man who was dreaming although his body and health showed as if nothing had happened to him in his life. Anyhow, I helped him to stand up and I took him to that room. I told him to sit on one stool which was in another part of that room, and then I first cut his hairs, moustache and beard very short, because all were overgrown and fearful to see. After, I cut all finger-nails quite short, then I took one of the big clothes which the woman or his wife, hung on the walls as part of decorations. He wrapped his body with it for the cloth which was on his body before was already torn into pieces for repeatedly beating by his wife.

After that, as he had then regained all his senses or was normal, both of us walked nearer to his wife who stood near one corner in that room. Then I forced her to surrender her supernatural power which she was using to change person into another form. She first refused to surrender it, but when she saw that I became so wild that I wanted to shoot her right out that moment, she vomited it in her both palms. It was just like a minute white bird. And it was shaking like a chicken which was just hatched. Then I took one of the calabashes which were in that room, she put it in it and then I covered that calabash with its lid before I put it in my hunting-bag because I was taking it to the town to show it to the people.

When it was about eight o'clock in the morning, I was taking this woman and her husband to the town. But when I took them to the town and the people saw them in front of me, her husband was snatched with gladness by the people and was carried by head to his father's palace, although his wife was stoning along in the town until we came to the palace.

When I took her to the king (the father of her husband) and then I told him how I had saved his son and again, I gave him the supernatural power of that woman, which she had vomited. And when the king removed the cover of the calabash and saw it, he gave the order to take the woman to the god of iron in the front of the palace. Therefore she was tied up to a tree in front of the god.

The king and his chiefs thanked me greatly for saving his son. In the following morning, several ceremonies were started which lasted for many days. After the ceremonies had been performed, the king fulfilled his promise. He gave me many costly clothes, costly coral beads and many costly presents which I brought to the village and I sold them for a considerable amount of money.

"And that was the end of the entertainment of this night, my people, or the end of the adventure of my second journey. So tomorrow, I shall continue to tell you the adventure of my third journey!"

Then after the people beat the drums, sang, and danced for a few minutes they went back to their houses with gladness.

I was Caught by the Savage Men

The entertainment of the fourth night

(*My third Journey*)

Now the people of my village were gathered in the front of my house. They were even increased by seventy-five per cent, because news had reached almost all the rest villages which were near, that I was telling the stories of my past adventures in form of entertainments. When some of the people had seated and those who had no chairs stood round us. Then everyone was served with the palm-wine and the biggest keg was in front of me. So after the drums were beaten and the people danced for about one hour as they were drinking the palm-wine. Then I started to tell the story of my third adventure as follows:

After a few days that I had returned from my second journey to the village with a lot of valuable treasures, I bought three puppies and I started to tame them in such a way that within a few days they had become as wild as a tiger. I bought those dogs in respect of my journeys for I had needed dogs' help greatly in all of my past journeys. The names were given to each of them according to its action and cleverness. The name of the first was "Sweeper" because it always ate without any remnant, the name of the second was "Cutter" because it was so bold, fast and wild that it always cut its victim or any dangerous animals into pieces and the name of the third was "Swallower" because it never chew neither bones nor anything before swallowing them.

Then with my dogs, gun and matchet, I started to hunt in

the forests which were not so far away from the village. With the help of my dogs, I used to kill several animals in one day. So my father, mother, sister and my junior brother, Alabi, were enjoying our lives with the every animal that I killed. But for that enjoyment, I determined not to go to another journey until after one year. Of course, I had forgotten that all the monies which I had saved would soon finish if I did not work hard for more.

During the period that I was in the village, almost all the people of the village were coming to my house to eat and drink from the morning till the late hour in the night. And many of the people told me that they would follow me to my next journey but they were discouraged when I told them the punishment, hardships, danger, etc. of it.

In the very month that I completed one year since when I had returned from my second journey. One fine night, at about eight o'clock I took my usual gun, matchet and after I hung my hunting-bag on my shoulder. Then I bade good-bye to my father, mother, sister and brother and then I left the village for the town of the savage people. That town was far away and I had been hearing from the old people that the people were very rich in all things but no man who would go there and return. They said that the savage people were so cruel that even none of the animals in their bush could be killed or taken away by any hunter, however he might be bold and strong.

But of course, since when I had heard that the people were very rich, I made up my mind that night to go there, not for animals but for the treasures. But I had made a great mistake, I left my three dogs in the village. I thought they would not be able to see well as it was in the night. Of course, my mother had advised me to take them along with me but I rejected her advice.

Having travelled in the darkness till about two o'clock in

the morning, I came to the forest in the middle of which that savage people lived. Having travelled deeply in it, then I stopped behind a rock. I sat down and I was resting for I was very tired before reaching there. As I was still resting and thinking in mind of what to do before I could get some of the treasures of that savage people, I did not know when I leaned on that rock and I fell asleep at the same time. But as I was dreaming of the man who had been transformed into half-snake by his wife, the man that I had saved when I went my second journey. There I felt suddenly a heavy knock on my forehead. The knock was so painful that I dazed and fell down at the same time. But as a brave man should do, I hastily stood up and ready to shoot my gun. But as I was about to shoot the gun, there I saw a tall black shadow. The shadow held my gun downward and then within that moment it gave me a slap on the face suddenly, and my gun sprang to a short distance.

Of course, as I put all my hope only on this gun, so I ran to it at the same time. As I bent down and I was just trying to pick it up, the fearful shadow had come nearer to my back and as I was standing up. The shadow pushed me from back and I turned somersault suddenly several times within that moment. However, I hastily stood up with the gun in hand and it was that time I saw clearly who was ill-treating me like that. The shadow turned into a very tall old woman immediately I stood up. She was very strong and tall like a giantess, she was very rough in appearance, neither of her arms was very long and strong, and so every one of her feet was long and thick, the hair of her head was long, dirty and scattered roughly like that of a mad person and her both breasts were nearly touching the ground.

As I stood before her, my height hardly reached one-sixth of her height. But when I raised up my head just to ask from her why she had treated me so badly like that. I noticed that she franked both eyes, she was in excess anger and was murmuring with great annoyance. When I saw her in that fearful action, I could not ask anything from her again. So I simply stood before her and I was looking at her with fear.

After a while, when she started to push my nose with finger and was murmuring repeatedly: "What do you come to do in this forest by this hour! Have you ever seen a person like you to come here! You people will disturb us in the day and so in the night!" Then I was walking backward slowly but I did not turn my back towards her because it had just revealed to me that she was not a human being but a dangerous night creature. But as I was walking backward with fear, she was also walking slowly towards me and was still pushing my nose with her thick finger.

At last, when my nose was going to burst soon, I thought in mind that if I did not defend myself at that stage, the hideous night woman would kill me soon. Therefore, I struck her forehead with my gun instead to shoot it to her because I feared whether they were many and if the rest heard the sound of my gun might rush out to kill me.

To my surprise and fear, my gun was hardly struck her forehead when she said loudly: "Ah! ah! ah! you beat immortal night woman!" And then she stretched one hand to her right and rooted out one slender stick and without hesitation, she was beating me from head to feet repeatedly. As she was beating me and I was striking her head with my gun, it was so she was repeating: "Ah, immortal beat you this night and so you will die soon!" So it was that night I knew that immortal creatures were not to be beaten by human being.

At last, when I was quite sure that she was stronger than me and if she continued to beat me so severely for some minutes more, I would die. Then I left her to strike with the gun but I started to run away for my life in the darkness but yet, she was chasing me along and beating me with all her power and so she was saying: "You are mortal, so you can die but I am immortal therefore, I cannot die!"

When I heard her saying so, I became more afraid and I ran to one mighty tree which was nearby. I hardly started to climb it along when she ran to it and continued to beat me but that did not prevent me to climb it along. She tried to pull me down but was late to do so because I had then climbed the tree far away. And as she stood at the bottom thinking what to do to bring me down to her, I had got to the top of the tree and sat on one of its branches and I was looking at her faintly at the bottom.

After she had failed in all her efforts to bring me down, then she went away. But when I had waited for some minutes and did not see her to return, I thought she would not come back to me and I was very happy about that. Unfortunately, as I was just climbing the tree down, there I saw that she was coming back and two strong men with big axes in hands were following her. Then I hastily climbed back to the same branch.

Immediately she brought the two men to that tree and pointed me to them and they saw me on top of that tree. They started to cut it as hastily as they could although it had several big buttresses. But when I believed that I would die immediately it fell down or if I did not die, the night woman and her men would tear me into pieces if they could catch me. So this critical moment forced me to remember my mother's advice. For she had told me to take my three dogs along with me before I had left the village and I blamed myself greatly for it.

Then with perplexity, I stood up right on top of the tree and I hopelessly called with the topmost of my voice: "My dogs! My dogs! My dogs! The Cutter, the Sweeper, the Swallower! Let all of you come to this forest now!" It was like that I was calling my dogs by their names with fear without stopping. I wondered that the dogs were hearing the call and were trying to come to me but unfortunately they were in their room that time and the door of that room was already locked up when my people had wanted to sleep.

After they had struggled and failed to get the way out, then they started to bark loudly and were running to and fro until their noises woke my mother. So she opened the door and they went out. As I was still calling them and they were running to that forest with all their power, those two men had cut the tree to the stage that it was shaking slightly to fall down and that night woman was ready to snatch me whenever it fell. A few minutes later, I lose my hope, because the tree was then preparing to fall down. But as I was still calling my dogs perplexedly, there I saw them running here and there in that forest, they were finding me about and they hardly come to the tree when I incited them to the two men and the night woman.

To my great joy, they were hardly saw me on top of that tree when they rushed against them. The men tried to cut them with their axes but my dogs did not give them chance but they were biting them instead. At last, they escaped with the night immortal woman and my dogs drove them far away before they came back to me and I had come down from that tree then.

Then I left that area with my dogs for another part of the forest. I lay down helplessly till the morning because that immortal woman had beaten me too much, but I was not discouraged at all to continue my journey to the town of the savage people.

In the following morning, I started to roam about in that forest in search for that town. But to my surprise, I found nothing like a town in that forest. When I roamed till about one o'clock midday then I stopped under the shadow of a tree. Having rested for a while, I went further and my dogs killed one animal which I roasted immediately. I ate some of it and I gave the rest to my dogs. Not knowing that there was no real town in that forest for those savage people but their inhabitations were the holes of the rocks which were common to be seen everywhere in that forest. And they were not coming out in the day-time except in the night. So I rested till the night when this revealed to me.

In the following night, I started to roam about with my dogs. After a while, I was seeing them everywhere in the forest and so they were troubling me just to leave there but I did not leave there until when they became entirely annoyed and then they chased me to kill. When I climbed a tree and hid in its leaves they failed to catch me. Having tried all their efforts to trace me out but failed, then they went away. And it was not so long when I fell asleep on that tree while my dogs slept at the bottom. My intention was to continue my journey in the following morning to another part of the world having failed to find any treasure in that forest.

To my fear was that, when it was about two hours that I was sleeping, I woke suddenly by the barks of my dogs. Then I peeped down to see what was happening to them, but I saw that all of them were tied up together with a single rope to one nearby tree. They were struggling to cut that rope but they could not do it. But when I was preparing to come down to see who was ill-treating them like that, there I saw clearly this time that over five hundred of the savage people sat round that tree. Then without hesitation, I hid back in the leaves and they did not suspect that I was on top of that tree. Not knowing that the bottom of that tree was the place of their meeting and they came there that night to make an important meeting. I wondered that my dogs did not wake until when they were tied up to the tree.

I saw through the flame of the fire which was glaring in the centre of their circle, that many of them were seriously sat down, many were arguing within themselves so seriously that they were preparing to beat themselves, fighting weapons were in the middle of them. Their attitudes showed that there was a serious misunderstanding between them and that they gathered under that tree and were waiting for their king to come and settle it.

After they had waited for about one hour but their king did not come out. One of them stood up, he shouted loudly: "Oh, the king of the savage people, why not you attend to the meeting, this night? Are you sick? The skull of man is your drinking vessel! The bones of man are your walking-stick, etc! Come out! Come out! Come now, we are waiting for you!" After the flatterer had flattered their king like that, then he (king) shouted so terribly and loudly that his voice shook the hills, rocks and trees and all the animals in that forest were so feared that they became mutes, all birds woke in their nests and all the rest living creatures were so feared that they were unable to move their bodies but stood still as if they had died.

After a few minutes that the king had shouted like that, I saw him when he was coming out from one mighty rock which was not so far from that tree. He was walking with the walking-stock which was made with man's bones and his bearer carried one big skull of human being with one chair and he was following him to that meeting. When both of them came to the meeting, the chair was put in the centre of the circle and when he sat on it then that skull was put down before him and he rested his feet on it. Then the bearer went to his back and he stood there as if he was keeping watch of him. After that the king shouted very loudly and terribly as before. But his voice shook that tree so heavily that I fell on him suddenly without my wish.

This was a great danger to me, because the king was badly wounded and his chair was partly damaged beyond repair.

So I admitted at the same time that the next thing that they would do was to kill me immediately. As many of them were scrambling me not to run away it was so the rest were scrambling their king and were taking care of him not to hurt more. At last when he became normal, he ordered one who was next to him in rank, the senior chief, to take me to his house and to bring me back to the meeting, which was postponed to five days' time, to be killed. After that he cancelled the meeting of that night and then every one went back to his house. But they left my dogs tied up and I was not quite sure whether they forgot to loose or kill them before they had left there.

So the senior chief was pushing me along to his house and so he was ill-treating me along. After we had travelled in both darkness and rays of the moon for about one hour, he came to his house at about three o'clock in the morning. After he had pushed me in, he shut the entrance with one heavy stone and then he continued to push me along.

His house was the hole of a vast rock. It was a long and deep hole which was just like a mighty building. There were several huge holes on both sides which were just like rooms. After a while he pushed me to the room in which he was sleeping. But before he entered the room, he took my gun, he leaned it near the entrance of that room and he took my hunting-bag and hung it near the gun. Then he took the matchet and flung it away but I hastily followed it with eyes and I saw where it fell. Having done all that, he stretched hand to one corner nearby, he brought out one big chain, he put it on my neck and then tied up the second end of it to one heavy stone. When he was quite sure that I could not escape, he entered the room. He lighted up the room and then took some shots of drink. Having rested for a while, he walked back to the door, he looked at me and murmured for a few minutes before he walked back, then he lay down and slept.

Through the light, I saw clearly that there were many pots

of corals, raw gold and silver, money, expensive beads, etc. but I did not know where he had got them. Having seen all these treasures, I breathed out heavily. I thought of two things, how to save my life from him and how to take some of that treasures away.

When I noticed well that he had slept deeply and I was hearing him snoring loudly, I started to strike the chain with a stone perhaps it would break away from my waist but all my efforts were in vain. Again, I attempted to walk to the place that he hung my hunting-bag and the gun to take them but the chain was too short to allow me to reach there. At last, I left myself to what was going to happen to me in that hole.

This senior chief of the savage people woke when it was about six o'clock in the morning. After he had stretched every part of his body, he walked to the light, he put more oil in the lamp and then he walked to the corner in which there were many kinds of hot drinks. After he had taken several shots from each, he came to me, he pressed every part of my body as if he was a doctor. After that he loosened the chain away from my waist, he fastened a string of leather to my neck but in such a way that if he pulled it, it would choke my throat immediately. Having done that, he took one leather whip and then forced me to bend down and without mercy, he jumped on my back. He held the string of my neck with left hand and then started to ride me about in that hole like a horse. It was like that I started my punishment in that hole.

After a while I became tired to be carrying him about and I stopped to rest. But he flogged me and then pulled up the string of my neck so tightly that I was unable to breathe. So willing or not I continued to carry him about. As he was on my back, it was so he was scratching my body with his long and sharp nails. Sometime, he was jumping up and down on my back and it was so he was shouting and laughing very loudly. And my back was wetted with his spat which was dropping down in large quantity as he was doing all these things.

When the punishment was too severe for me to bear, I cried for help but there was nobody to render any help. I called my dogs loudly but they were unable to come, because they were already tied up. At last, I started to beg this cruel senior chief, but the more I begged him the more he flogged me. When I did not know what to do again and I was entirely tired, that moment, I wilfully fell down, with the hope that if I did so he would come down from my back. But it was that time he held the projection of my throat and then he pressed it so hardly that I stood up suddenly and continued to carry him about.

After a while, I hid my pains but I started to sing a kind of song which I believed he, as one of the savage people, would like to hear or perhaps he would leave me when he heard it. But to my disappointment, I hardly started to sing that song when he took part in it. When I sang it in tenor, he sang it in bass. When I sang it in bass, he sang it in treble with great joy. But I blamed myself at last to form that song, because it added to my punishment instead to lessen it. For as he was singing it with me, he was just doing as if he was crazy. He enjoyed it so much that he had lost all his senses at the same time and he was jumping up so highly that his head was striking the roof of that hole. And he rode me to the roughest part of the hole which he had avoided before.

When he rode me till twelve, he went down from my back, he chained me near the door of his room and after he had loosened the string of my neck, he entered the room. After a while, he came back with some unripened bananas and he threw them on my head. But he hardly threw them on me when I snatched them and swallow all even quicker than to swallow my spat, because I was already nearly to die of hunger.

Having taken his own food which was meat and drunken many shots from each of all the drinks which were hung in the corner of his room, he lay down on the mat of corals and then he fell asleep. I sat down and leaned my back on the rock nearby. As I was thinking in mind that if I failed to escape, he would ride me to death soon or if he did not ride me to death before their next meeting, no doubt, they would kill me in the meeting. But as sleep was just as death, so I did not know when I fell asleep unnoticed.

As I was still sleeping with pains, he woke up. He walked to where I was and when he saw me that I was sleeping, he was so annoyed that he kicked me on the back. When I woke and stood up suddenly, he gave me several slaps on the face before he walked back to his room. I was very lucky that he did not ride me for the rest part of that day and I did not see him until when he was going out in the night. When he went out he closed the main entrance back with usual heavy stone, so that I might not go out or escape before he returned.

When he came back in the morning, he loosened the chain away, from my waist, he put the usual string of leather on my neck, he held the usual whip and then he mounted my back and started to ride me to and fro. But as my power could not carry him along as quickly as I had done the previous day and that I began to fall down continuously, because I was so tired that I could not even lift myself up. So instead to come down from my back, this cruel man held my head and throat with all his power and simply kept quiet.

At last, when I could not breathe well and I was dying, then having struggled for a few minutes, I stood up and he continued to ride me along without mercy. With extreme pains, I did not know when I began to call my dogs so loudly that they heard my call. But when they heard my call they struggled so hard that the rope with which they were tied up cut, because before that time it had already dried up by the heat of the sun. And within a few minutes, they ran to that rock but unfortunately, they could not enter into it because the entrance was shut with a heavy stone by that cruel man. As I was still calling them loudly, they did not waste time at the entrance but they started to go around the rock, they were looking for another entrance.

But as this cruel man had seen my dogs before me he hastily covered my mouth with his thick palm, so that I might not be able to shout again. But of course, I was still struggling with him to take his palm away from my mouth. My dogs climbed the rock to the top, then they jumped into that hole through the small round space which was on top of it. They hardly jumped in when they rushed to him and began to bite him so severely that he jumped away from my back without his wish.

When he bent down and was just picking up one stone with which to beat them, they rushed to him again and they bit both his head and eyes so severely that he fell down powerlessly at the same time. And without hesitation, I started to beat him with a heavy stone which I found nearby. When I believed that he had no more power to revenge on me that time. I walked round the hole and I found my matchet from where he had thrown it. Again, I went to his door, I took my gun and hunting-bag and after that I went back to him. I was threatening him with my gun to give me some of his treasures. When he agreed to do so, I dragged him to his room and he allowed me to take some of each. So I took some of the raw gold, silver, coral and many other saleable articles. After that I went out of that rock with my dogs. But if he had not agreed to give me some of his property, I would not attempt to take them for I did not like to be an extortioner.

Having carried all these treasures to the village, the people rushed to my father's house to witness them and were very surprised when I sold all for a lot of money, but they did not know that I had been severely punished before I got them. But I was honoured greatly by the old people of the village because they knew that if a person was not bold and brave enough and again to be able to endure severe punishment, the savage people would kill him. So I stayed in the village with my people for six months before I went to another town, when the dry season was just started.

After the people had listened to the story of my third adventure, they beat the drums, danced, sang, and drank the palm-wine for a while before every one went back to his or her house in the midnight.

From the Town of Famine to the Town of the Water People

The entertainment of the fifth night

(*My fourth Journey*)

In the fourth night, when the people gathered in the front of my house and the drinks were served as they were dancing and singing with great joy. Then I stopped them and I addressed them first as follows: "I am very happy indeed to see all of you again in front of me and I thank every one of you for the true affection you have on me, although I am the head of the village. And I wonder greatly too to see that you are increased again this night more than ninety per cent. But (all sat quietly and paid great attention to me) when I first saw the whole of you, I was afraid, but after I thought it over again my fear was expelled. Because I first thought within myself that where to get sufficient planks to make coffins for every one of you when you die because you are too many. But when I thought it over again, I remembered that not the whole of you would need coffins to bury you when you die. Because many of you would be killed and eaten up by the wild animals. Many would die in the rivers, many would be burnt into ashes by the fire, many would be kidnapped and so many of you would be fallen into the wells. So therefore, coffins would not be required for those who died such death, and so many would not die in their homes but where their people would not see their bodies to bury with coffins." But the people were greatly annoyed when they heard like that from me. All were snapping their fingers on heads and saying that they would not die in the rivers or in the fire or in the wells or eaten up by the wild animals, but they would die in their homes, villages, etc., and they would be buried with coffins. But after a while, when their noises went down, I explained to them that they must not misunderstand me, because there was nobody on earth who could know the real place and real time he or she is going to die, or if anyone knew, let him or her tell me. And if anyone knew it, it meant I was guilty of what I had said. Having said so, I hesitated to hear the reply but there was none of the people who could reply but they admitted at last.

After they danced and drank some of their palm-wine, I started to tell them the story as follows:

One fine morning, after six months that I had returned from my third journey, I took my usual gun, hunting-bag and matchet. I bade good-bye to my father, mother, sister and brother and all my friends and my neighbours. Some of the people cautioned me very seriously not to go for any treasure again. They said that all I had brought were enough. But I told them that I must try more for we knew of today but we did not know of tomorrow.

Then I left my village that bright day and I was going to the north this time. Having travelled for several days, I came to a town. This town was very big and famous. It was near a very wide and deep river. Immediately I entered the town, I was greatly shocked first with fear when I saw the terrible appearances of the people or the inhabitants. Every one of them was so leaned that he had no more muscle on his body. Every one of them was as thin as a dried stick. The legs and arms were just like sticks. The eyes were seeing faintly in the skull except the head which was so big that the thin neck could not even carry it. Both upper and lower jaws had already dried up like a roasted meat. The stomach was no more seen except the breast and exposed ribs.

When I first saw them in that appearances, I thought within myself and cried out unnoticed: "Ah, how people were created so terribly like this?" Because in the first instance I did not know that they were in famine and that they were starved until when they had leaned to that state. And they were so starved that the breasts of the women had dried up. The king too was so bitterly starved that he was unable to put on his crown whenever he went out. And it was a great pity that the hunger had forced the people of the town not to respect the king or chiefs again except one who brought food to them.

But according to the custom of that town, I was first taken to the king and when he approved of my staying there, then I lodged in the house of the paramount chief which was almost next to the palace of the king. When it was night I tried to sleep but I was unable to fall asleep because of hunger. So hardly in the morning when I went to the king and told him: "Please king, I am badly hungry, will you give me something to eat now?" But he said at the same time: "Is that so? Sorry, we are in great famine since past few years, therefore, I have no food to give you except cold water which is our main food in this town at present!"

Then I went back to my room, I sat and I was expecting that the paramount chief would soon send food to me as the king had failed to give it to me. Having waited for many hours and yet he did not send anything to me. Then I sold my shame and I went to him. Without shame, I told him that I wanted to eat. But he said that their main food was cold water. He said furthermore that the famine was so serious that they had money but it was useless. They had plenty of costly clothes but the hunger did not let them wear them and even the clothes were oversized them because they had leaned too much. And again, this paramount chief advised me that I should be drinking the cold water.

Having heard like that as well from him, then without hesitation, I started to drink the cold water. But when it was not yet daybreak when I was woken by hunger in the following morning. I hardly got up when I went to the king's attendants, I complained to them again that since I had come to the town I had nothing to eat except cold water which I was drinking. I complained to them perhaps they might help me. But I was very surprised that they did not allow me to tell them all of my complaints when they interrupted immediately they heard the word "hunger" from me. They naked themselves and told me to look how every one of them was leaned. They told me further that I too would soon become bones if I kept longer in that town.

Having failed again to get food from the attendants, I shook my head with surprise before I left them. When I returned to my room, I sat down quietly and I began to think how to get food by all means. I first thought to go back to my village to be bringing the food stuffs to this town for sale. But I remembered that my village was too far away from there and again, there was no real road on which to be travelled always.

As I was still suggesting within myself of what to do, it came to my mind to go to the big river which was near this town, perhaps I might get fishes from there. And without hesitation, I went to that river. Luckily, I found many canoes tied up to the trees on the bank and I loosened one. I put my matchet in it and then I pushed it on the river. I started to find fishes about to kill. But there was none to be found. But of course, as I was still paddling along, I came to the swampy bush at about twelve o'clock p.m. In that swampy bush, there were many palm-trees. When I stopped the canoe, I climbed one palm-tree but unfortunately, there was no fruits on it. But when I climbed the third one, I found two ripen bunches of palm-fruits on top of it. So I drove all the birds which were eating them away first and then I cut both down.

After I had put them in the canoe, I first ate of them to my satisfaction and then I took the rest to the town. But I was nearly torn into pieces by the hungry people as I was carrying them along in the town to the king. However, I carried them to the king at last. With great wonder and admiration, he took them from me and thanked me greatly. Having eaten as many fruits as he could then he distributed the rest to his people.

After the people had gone back to their houses, the king invited me to one of his property rooms. He showed me all his money and many other property as gold, silver, costly beads and diamonds. He promised me that if I could be getting such palm-fruits for him and his people till when the famine was finished, he would give me a lot of money, gold, silver, diamond and beads as rewards. Having promised me like that, I replied with a smile that I would try my best to be supplying him the fruits till when the famine was finished and then I went back to my room, in the paramount chief's house.

In the following morning, I went to the river again. I tried all my efforts in climbing so many palm-trees. Luckily after a while, I got one bunch of palm-fruits and I brought it to the king. After he had eaten of the fruits to his satisfaction he distributed the rest to his people. It was so I brought the fruits to the king and his people for the period of five months. But unfortunately, as the famine was not stopped in time and the season of the palm-fruits came to an end, therefore, I could not get anything for the king any more. I tried all my best to get the fruits but it was in vain.

When it was the third day that I had not eaten except to drink the cold water from morning till night, I was so weak that I thought that I would die soon. I thought of going back to my village that time but I could not trek the distance of about one mile when I would fall down. This my fourth journey was so bad and hopeless that I said within myself that if I returned to my village this time I would never attempt to go for any treasure again.

Having failed in all my efforts to get food, then I went back to the palm-trees perhaps I might get some fruits which probably had fallen to the bottoms of the palm-trees during the season. So I started to search the bottom of every palm-tree and I found only one over ripen fruit when it was about three o'clock in the afternoon. I hastily picked it up. But as I held it, I said to myself sorrowfully that what a single palm-fruit could do for me. It could not satisfy my hunger.

Anyhow, I went in the canoe. But as I was paddling it along on the river and when I came to the deepest part of it, this palm-fruit was mistakenly fallen into the water. And this was affected me so badly that I threw the paddle in the canoe and then jumped in the water without hesitation. But as I was swimming here and there just to pick up the fruit, someone held my both feet and was pulling me down into the bottom of the river. Having tried all my best to take my feet from him and failed then I left myself to him. After a while he pulled me into the water and it was then I saw who was pulling me. He held one coffin, with left hand. The lid of that coffin was glass and he hardly pushed that lid to one side when he pushed me in it and he entered it as well and then covered it with that glass lid at the same time. As I was inside the coffin with him, I was breathing in and out quite easily and I saw plainly that this man covered his body from the knee to the waist with the leather of big fish. He had no hair on head but small scales instead, his arms were very short and were as strong as iron but there were fingers on each arm and they were resembled that of human being. Although he had two eyes like myself but each was as round as full moon.

But to my fear, he had fins on shoulders, elbows, knees and ankles and there were a number of moustache on his upper jaw, which was that of a big fish. His mouth was flat but the nose was round. As the coffin was taking us deeply into the river, this man began to threat me badly. Sometime, he would scratch my face with his sharp nails, sometime he would slap me on the ear and sometime he would be frightening by pointing a sharp iron on my eyes. It was like that he was ill-treating me until the coffin took us to the bottom of the river. Then he pushed the lid of the coffin to one side, he came down and then pulled me out. When I came down, I noticed that we were on the land and not in the water as before. The river was seen no more. Then he pushed me in front of him and told me to be going along on one road which led to a very beautiful house. As I was going along it was so he was following me as fast as he could.

On both sides of that road, there were beautiful trees and flowers. Having travelled on that road for a while, I was seeing several men similar to this one, they lined up on both sides of the road as if they were policemen or soldiers. Having travelled further, we came to the front of that beautiful house. And it was then I saw it clearly that it was a mighty palace. As he was escorting me along in it and as we were going from one place to another, I was seeing the costly decorations which were hung on every corner. Again, I noticed the sun was so dull that there was only little difference from the full moon of the dry season. The air was a little thicker than my village's air and the sands on the ground were as white as white cloth. The sky was almost cloudy throughout the day.

After a while, that man escorted me to the beautiful sitting-room in which one beautiful lady sat in royal state. Without hesitation, I stood before her and bowed down as the man who had escorted me in stood at back. But when I stood for a few minutes, I simply walked to one of the seats and then sat on it. Hardly crossed my legs when I started to glance at every decorations which were on the walls and on the floor. Now it was revealed to me that the inhabitants of this town were the water people and that beautiful lady was the nymph of that river, so they were belonged to the fish race. The nymph and her attendants and guardsmen were very surprised as I was not afraid of them at all, but they did not know that I had surrendered myself to all what might happened to me that time.

The decorations on the walls were stuffed gold fishes, polished large sea shells, skulls of the sea animals, etc. and every part of that walls was twinkling like stars. The seats were also stuffed fishes and were as fresh as if they were still alive. The ruler or the nymph herself was dressed in the skins of beautiful fishes. The skins were so highly refined that they were as smooth as very costly clothes. Some were shining like gold, some were twinkling like the bright stars and the top ones were shining steadily like diamonds. She sat on an arm-chair which had many carved sea creatures on top. She stretched feet on a well-polished skull of a big whale. Many big sea tortoises were walking about on the floor and the crown on her head was full of small beautiful sea shells.

As far as I saw her, she was about thirty years old. Her eyes were very clear and the face was very fresh as the face of a fifteen-year-old girl. There were no scars or pimples on her cheeks or face and the hair of her head was not so much dark but of course, probably the climate of that town had turned the hair to be like that. Her teeth were very white and very closely to each other. Her nose was quite pointed like that of an image, the slippers on her feet were made from the soft leather of crocodile. She had clear and lovely voice and her face always seemed as if she was kind and merciful.

As I was still noticing all these things, a number of another set of guardsmen walked in and those whom I met in there walked out and those who were just come in took over the duty. Again, I noticed these new set of the guardsmen that everyone of them was a man of strong body, stout and fearful to see. The skull of shark was on everyone's head, and wore the apron which was the skin of fish but the scaly skins of fishes were their purtises and gloves. Many of them held the tails of big fishes. Each of that tails was about four feet long and the width was about six inches and very thick indeed and sharp thorns were lined up on both edges. Some of those who held the long spears were shielded their breasts with the very big sea tortoise back shells. All of these were their uniforms. Every one of them was a giant-like and cynical.

As I sat on the chair facing the nymph or the queen of the river and I was still looking at the decorations and thinking also in mind that no doubt I would leave this town with much wealths, the man who had brought me in there started to complain to the nymph that he brought me before her for punishment because I struck his head when I jumped on the river when the only palm-fruit which I could find had fallen into the river. That man hardly complained to the nymph when all her guardsmen gathered at my back and ready to hold me. But the nymph hastily rang the bell on her side, to them to leave me. Then with a very cool voice, she asked from me: "Why did you strike him on the head?" So before I started to reply, I first crossed my feet and seated very easy as if I was in my house and then I said: "In fact, I jumped on the river when the only palm-fruit that I could get, had fallen in the water. But I did not know whether I had struck him on the head but if it was so then it was by a mistake." She asked again: "Why did you jump into the river in respect of one palm-fruit?" And as those guardsmen were in attention and got ready to hold me if the nymph gave them the order to do so. So I replied: "My work was to find the palm-fruits to the people of the town of famine because they had nothing to eat since the famine had started in their town and they had already leaned to the bones." But when she heard like that from me, she was so wondered that she sat up and then asked again: "The famine was so serious that only the palm-fruits the people eat?" I said: "Yes. Even the palm-fruits were not easily to get." Then she and her guardsmen breathed out with wonder and as she hesitated and was looking at me the guardsmen looked at each other's eyes with great wonder and then stood easy and that showed me that they were in sympathy with me. So the nymph said suddenly: "Oh, no wonder, your appearance even shows that you are in a great famine because you are too lean." But I hastily interrupted: "That town is not mine but I went there to find the treasure."

But as she was about to ask me another question, one beautiful lady walked in that moment. She put one big basin in front of her and then she bowed down for her and walked out. When she removed the lid of that basin, it was roasted fish and then she started to eat it as a refreshment. But as I was very hungry even before I was brought before her, so I stood up, I walked to her and without excuse, I took some slices and then I walked back to my seat and there I started to eat the fish bit by bit with greediness. But as the nymph was kind and merciful, she rang the bell on her side and after a few seconds, one attendant walked in. Then she told her to take me to the dining-room and give me food. So I walked out with that attendant. She (attendant) gave me the nice food which I ate to my entire satisfaction. After that I went back to the nymph. Having discussed with me about the famine for a while, she stood up and walked into one room opposite that sitting-room. After a while she came back with one round box. It was very big but one man could carry it from one place to another. It was sealed round. She gave it to me and then explained to me that, "This sealed box (she pointed finger to it) will supply food and drinks of all kinds to you and the people of the town of famine throughout the period of the famine. But you and the people must be very careful not to break the delicate box. If you break it it will not be able to supply anything to you any more and all of you will be punished for it. Furthermore, if it is stolen away from you, all of you will be punished as well. And again, you must put in your mind always that you must not come back to me for anything as from today!"

Having warned me like that she rang the bell and the man (the water-man) who had brought me to her, walked in. As he stood before her, she told him to take me back to where he had caught me. Then I put the box on head, I thanked her greatly before I followed the water-man and some of the guardsmen led us to a short distance before they went back. After a while we came to where that coffin was. Having put that box in it and I went inside it, the water-man pushed it on to the river and then he entered it. But to my surprise, he hardly covered it with its lid when the coffin started to run furiously on the water and within a few seconds it floated on the very part of that river from which he had caught me before.

As my canoe was still driven here and there by the tides. Then as soon as the coffin stopped closely to it, I put that box in it and then I started to paddle it along to the town of famine. But that water-man did not talk to me until when he had brought me back to that river and returned to the nymph.

When I paddled the canoe for about two hours I reached the bank of that river. Having tied up the canoe, I carried the box direct to the king. In the presence of the paramount chief, the king removed the lid of it. To their surprise, they met several basins of variety of food and one small spoon in it. But they did not believe me when I told them that the food would be sufficient to feed the whole people till whenever the famine was finished.

Anyhow, the king put the box in his strong-room and he choose me to be serving the food to the people and to himself. Then I first served him and the paramount chief and they had first satisfied their hunger, then the whole people in the town were invited to the palace. The king told them that everyone of them should go back to his or her house and bring the plate and spoon. Then the people ran back to their houses and they returned with all these things after a few minutes. Then I began to serve each of them. But the people ate and drank to their satisfaction and yet the food and the drinks remained in that box as if I had not served from them.

It was so the people and the king were eating and drinking to their satisfaction for three times daily for three months and yet the food and the drinks remained as if nothing had touched them. And within a few weeks more, the people had forgotten the famine. They had enough muscles on bodies, they became as powerful as before the famine had started. They were able to walk about easily in the town, singing, dancing and laughing with great joy. They were so satisfied that they determined not to work again for their living.

But as the news of that wonderful box had spread to many towns and villages and many people from those towns and villages had come to witness that box. So one midnight, a gang of night marauders came from one of those towns to the palace. When they came in and as they were trying to break and enter into the strong-room to steal the box away to their town. The king's bugle-blowers who were keeping watch of the gate of the palace, started to blow the bugles just to wake the king and the rest people in the palace. When the people and the king woke, they took clubs, cudgels, matchets, axes, bows and arrows, etc. They rushed to the marauders and I followed them with my matchet in hand. Then all of us started to beat them but they beat us so mercilessly in return that everyone got wounds all over the body. They beat me until I fell down unconsciously. Every part of my body was bleeding continuously. But at last, when the arrows were shot to them continuously for a few minutes then they ran away for their lives.

After the marauders had escaped, the king and some of the rest people took me from the floor to one room. The king started to treat my wounds with medicine and all were healed within a few days. And the marauders did not attempt to come to the palace for some weeks, but one of them whom we did not recognize at all, came to the bugle-blowers. He tried all his possible best and made friends with them. He was so kind to them that they did not suspect him as one of the marauders. He was sitting with them from morning till the evening. He was just spying the easiest way to get into the strong-room in which the wonderful box was kept always.

Having satisfied himself, then he went back to his members and told them to be ready for another attempt to steal the box. In the very night that they were coming, he had come to the bugle-blowers before his members. He was playing with them as he was usually doing. But he hid one bottle of thick honey under his dress. When he noticed that the bugle-blowers went to the palace to take their supper, he hastily filled their bugles with that thick honey and then hung them back on their usual rack before they came back.

When they returned, he ate and drank with them, after that he told them that he was going to visit another man in the next house. But not knowing that immediately he had left them, he went direct to the rest marauders. He told them that it was time to go and bugle the strong-room. Then all of them came to the town and entered the palace through the other gate. As they were splitting the door of the strong-room with axes, the bugle-blowers woke and hastily took their bugles from the rack. But when put them in the mouths just to be blowing them as a warning to the king and the people in the palace that the night marauders came again. The thick honey started to run from their bugles into their mouths. Therefore, they were unable to blow the bugles but they were licking the honey and enjoying it as it was running into their mouths and it was so the marauders were breaking the strong-room as hastily as they could.

It was like that the room was broken into and the wonderful box together with the king's property were taken and then they left the town as quickly as possible. And they had gone far away before the bugle-blowers were able to blow their bugles after they had licked the honey in their bugles. Anyhow, the king and the rest people took up the fighting weapons. Then we chased the marauders to catch and then to take the box back from them. But they had gone too far away, we did not see any trace of them.

Then we came back to the palace. The king cast down on his throne and was thinking sorrowfully of what to eat in the morning. In the morning, when the people gathered in the front of the palace and were waiting for their breakfast, the king and his paramount chief told me to go back to the nymph for another wonderful box. But when I explained to the king that the nymph had warned me already not to come back to her for anything and she had warned me as well that if the box was split or stolen away, we would be punished for it. The hungry people shouted at a time: "Don't tell us a lie! But you must go back to her and if you explain to her how the box was stolen from the strong-room, she would not refuse to give you another one!" Again, I insisted to go back, but that time the king and the paramount chief said that if I refused to go back to the nymph it meant I disobeyed their order and therefore, they would punish me and the punishment was to behead me.

Anyhow, I went back to that river and as I was paddling the canoe along, I came to the same spot from where the water-man had taken me to the nymph the other day. Then I wilfully threw the paddle in the water with the hope that it would sink like that palm-fruit. But when the paddle did not sink, I jumped into the water and I hardly dived when the same water-man held my both feet and pulled me deeply into the water before he put me inside the same coffin and within a few minutes it took us to the town of the nymph. Then the water-man took me before her like the first time. He complained to her that he caught me again when I struck his head with my feet.

But the nymph grew annoyed when she saw me there again. Instead to say anything to the complaint of the water-man, she asked me: "Had I not told you last time not to come here again?" I replied with trembling voice: "In fact you had told me not to come to you again. But I come back to take another wonderful box in which everlasting food and drinks are kept!" Having heard like that from me, she became more anger and asked: "By the way, what has happened to the one which I had given to you the other day?" I replied that the night marauders had stolen it away from the king's strong-room a few days ago. Then she remarked with fearful voice: "Is that how you people are careless? I had warned you that you should keep the box so savely that it might not be stolen. All right, I shall send another thing to the king which will teach all of you sense!"

Then she stood up and entered the same room opposite the sitting-room and I was very happy when she told me that she would send another thing to us which would teach us sense. After a while she returned with one huge sealed pot. When gave it to me, she told me that I should open it when the whole people and the king gathered into one place. Then I thanked her greatly for I believed that this pot was going to supply the food and drinks like that box. So when I was ready to leave, she rang the bell to the same water-man and he walked in at the same time. As he bowed down for her, she told him to take me back with the same coffin. Having taken me back to where he had caught me, then I put the pot in my canoe and I paddled it to the bank and from there I carried the pot to the town.

The hungry people and the king who had already gathered in the front of the palace and were waiting for my return, shouted greatly with joy when they saw the pot on my head. But when I gave it to the king and he put it in the middle of the people, then I told him how he would open it. So he first told the people to bring their plates nearer and then he forced it open. But uncountable of bees, wasps and all kinds of the stinging insects rushed out from it instead of food and drinks. Without hesitation, these insects started to sting all of us. Within a few minutes many people were stung to death, that place was disordered at the same time. Everyone was running skelter helter for his or her life. And at last, as the king was running away for his life, the crown fell off from his head but he was unable to wait and take it back. So almost all the people of the town of famine had run away for their lives and when the town was empty, then I took my gun, hunting-bag and matchet and I started to go back to my village at the same time. I could not wait to tell the king to fulfil his promise but of course, he too was nowhere to be found.

After a few days' travel, I reached my village and I entered my father's house very quietly but not as joyfully as my last three journeys which had profited me greatly. Then the people rushed to my house to honour my return, but they were greatly shocked when they noticed that I did not bring anything this time. Having told them all what had happened to me in the town of famine, some cautioned me not to go any journey again and some advised me not to give up my adventures because time was not always as straight as a straight line and that one who was finding goodness about must endanger his life and must be able to endure all hardships as well. Then I thanked them greatly. After that I sent for drinks and all of us drank together till the midnight.

"That was the end of my fourth journey. It was so many journeys were not profitable in those days. One journey might prove to be a better one from beginning but might be the worst towards the end. But I was not discouraged at all as my fourth journey was vanity at last. I thank you for your listening. Good night to you all!" Then after the people of my village had danced, sung and drunken for a few minutes they went back to their houses.

The Goddess of the Diamonds on the Mountain

The entertainment of the sixth night

(*My fifth Journey*)

Now my people were gathered in front of my house to listen to the story of my fifth journey. After they were served with palm-wine and I drank some kegs. Then I sat right on my usual old arm-chair. I put fire in my pipe and as I was enjoying it, I started my story as follows:

Well, as I had told you last night that I was not discouraged at all to go to another journey, although I had helped the people of the town of famine but the end of my help was really bad and I left there with empty hands. But I continued my fifth journey after one year that I had returned from the town of famine. So immediately I woke up in that morning, I dressed up, I took my gun, hunting-bag and my usual matchet. After that I walked to my father's room, I bade him good-bye and so I did to my mother and then I set on my journey that morning.

After I had travelled for so many days, I came to a sea. This sea was so dangerous that several thousands of people were losing their lives in it every year when crossing it. It was in the north-east of my village. But those who had risked their lives and crossed it to the other side had returned with great fortunes and it were that fortunes had attracted me to attempt to cross it. When I waited on the bank of it for many days and yet there was no canoe with which to cross it. Then I started to travel along on its bank. After a while I saw one old canoe which had been driven on the weeds by the waves.

When I examined it, it had splitted from one end nearly to the other. But of course, I did not know whether the owner of it had been drowned in that sea and that was a great fear to me. But anyhow, I tied up the splitted part very securely with a rope. Having done that, I cut a twig of a big tree and carved it like a paddle. Then I hung my gun, hunting-bag and matchet on my shoulders, after that I pushed that canoe on the sea and then I was paddling it along.

To my surprise, and fear, I did not paddle it more than one mile when heavy rain and gale began. The gale was carrying my canoe deeply into the sea. I tried my best to paddle it back to the shore but all my efforts were failed. I was still in this restlessness of mind when the snows began to drop repeatedly. As I was protecting my head from the snows, the gale was carrying my canoe far away and as I was blaming myself that if I had known I should not had coveted to come to the sea, then the lightning started. Every part of the sea was so flashing that all the living creatures of the sea were in disorder within a few minutes.

As it was still raining heavily, then my clothes were soaked and all were stickened on to my body. Every part of my head was full of knobs for the snows which had struck it and after a while I could not see again, because the lightning was too powerful for the eyes to see anything. I shut my eyes and then left myself to this danger. But I hardly did so when my canoe broke into two and then I fell on the sea suddenly. But I was very lucky that my gun, hunting-bag and matchet were still with me and were dangling on my shoulders. After a while, my feet and hands were crambed and my teeth were striking each other for the cold.

When it was about two hours, the wave carried me to another shore which was closely to one mountain and I could only breathe in and out as I lay on the sands but I was unable to move any part of my body. I was still in this hardship when the lightning, wave and snows were stopped but to my surprise, all were hardly stopped when the sun continued. Although it was not so hot but I became conscious after a few hours it had heated up my body. Then I crawled to a short distance from the bank of the sea and with much difficulties, I collected some dried sticks and twigs which had fallen down from the top of that mountain.

I took out the two pieces of the flinty stones which were in my hunting-bag. So I began to strike one from the other just to produce fire on the dried sticks. I struck the two stones for several times but they failed to produce the fire. Having seen it like that, I was so embarrassed that I was about to kill my-self that moment, because without fire I could not eat any-thing which I might find near there and I could not be saved from the cold breeze of the sea. At last, without much hope, I tried again and luckily the stones produced fire this time.

When the whole dried sticks and the twigs were caught fire, then I took my clothes from my body, I hung them before the fire to dry. Having warmed my body well, I stood up, I walked back to the shore and I began to look for the edible things to eat but there was no any edible thing. I looked for the dead fishes but there were none as well. Then I came back to the fire. I sat sadly before it and I was thinking of the same thing—food. But at last, when the hunger did not let me stay in one place, I stood up, I went closely to the foot of that mountain and luckily there were a lot of crabs around there. I picked up as many as I wanted and then came back to the fire. I roasted them in the fire and ate them at the same time.

But as the time had gone and the darkness was approaching, so I did not attempt to climb the mountain that evening. When it was about ten o'clock in the night, I saw many lights faintly on top of that mountain and that showed me that a town was on top of it. I tried my best to see the top of it clearly but I was unable because it was so high that if a person raised his head up with hat on head to see the top of it, the hat on his head would certainly fall down yet he would not see it.

I had rest of mind when I saw that there was a town on top of that mountain and then I put hope to start to climb it in the following morning. But of course, I did not know yet whether the inhabitants of that town were persons like myself or they were spirits, ghosts or any other harmful creatures, but as I could not go back to my village from this place, therefore, I must go to that town to seek for help.

In the following morning, when it was about eight o'clock, I began to climb this vast mountain. But it was very hard for me to climb it to the distance of about one hundred feet because I was chasing about to kill by the wild animals like lions, tigers, apes, elephants, buffaloes, etc. and all kinds of birds of prey. These creatures were jumping very fiercely to everything that they saw climbing the mountain. As it was very dangerous to climb further, then I hastily discontinued just to save my life.

When I came back to the fire, I put more dried wood and then I began to warm my body. But within three days, I had eaten the whole crabs which were living at the bottom of the mountain and there was nothing for me to eat after that. At last, I was so much starved that I attempted to eat from the sands of the sea but I was unable to do so when I tasted it. Again, after some hours, when I was hungry to the climax, I attempted to eat from the leaves of the trees which were at the bottom of the mountain, but their juice was poisonous to the mouth.

In the afternoon of the fourth day that I had cast down powerlessly before the fire, there I felt a hot breath on my nape suddenly. The hot breath was just rushed on to my nape as if it was rushed out from the snout of an animal. I was greatly startled and trembled with fear and with trembling body, I looked at back suddenly. But to my surprise, I saw a very big camel with one small bag tied up to its neck. And without hesitation, I stood up and ran with fear to a short distance and then I was looking at it. But to my surprise, immediately it shook its neck to left and right, the bag fell down from its neck and then it began to run back to where it had come.

After it had gone away, I walked to that bag. When I loosened it, I saw yams, ripen plantains, bananas, four coconuts and one bottle full of the fresh water. Then I hardly thanked God when I put the yams in the fire and as they were roasting, I began to eat the bananas and plantains. But of course, as I was eating all these things, I was anxious greatly to know who was so kind in that sea to send them to me. And when the yams were roasted, I ate some of them and I kept the remaining near the fire to be warming. I drank from the fresh water to my satisfaction and then reserved the rest.

Having satisfied my hunger and thirst and had rest of mind, then I began to think once more who had sent those things to me. Although I knew that a merciful creature who had seen my hardships had sent them to me but I did not know where he or she was and then to go and meet him or her. Of course, after a while it came to my mind that if the camel came to me again, I would follow it to where it was coming to me, and then I got ready to do so. In the following day, God was so good, it came again with another kinds of food stuffs. But before the usual bag dropped from its neck, I hastily mounted it and without hesitation it was carrying me back to where it had come.

When it travelled far away on the shore, it began to climb that mountain to the top. Having climbed it to the summit on which there was a very beautiful town, it took me direct to the main gate of that town. As the gate was closed that time, it waited for a few minutes. As I was on its back it was so I was stretching out my neck to see this town before the gate would be opened, just to know whether to get down from its back from that place if the inhabitants were dangerous, but unfortunately, I could not see it because it was entirely surrounded with high and thick walls.

As I was still stretching my neck to see the inhabitants, the gate was opened suddenly by one beautiful lady. Then the camel walked in and the gate was shut back and she was following it as it was carrying me along in the town. And as I was on its back, I noticed that this town was very clean, camels were commonly seeing everywhere, and the houses were very beautiful and very big. The men were very few but beautiful ladies were outnumbered the men in great number.

It was not so long when that camel carried me to the biggest building and then it stopped near the entrance of that building and was hesitating for me to get down from its back. But as I was on its back and I was still looking at everywhere with great wonder and fear, the lady who had followed it to that building, pulled me down suddenly. As I fell down, my gun, bag and my matchet fell away from my shoulders. But as I was scrambling them, my finger touched the trigger of the gun and then it (gun) fired so loudly that all the inhabitants rushed out with fear. That lady fell down and nearly fainted for fear.

Anyhow, when she became conscious, and as I was about to run away, she and some of the rest people caught me and then they dragged me into that building as if I were a thief. This building belonged to the Goddess of Diamonds. Then I was taken to the goddess who sat in her beautiful court. And before that lady began to complain to her, I hastily bowed down for her and then stood in attention like a brave soldier while my gun, hunting-bag and the matchet were on my both shoulders. Then the lady complained that I was brought to the town by one of their camels and then, I wilfully shot my gun in the town.

Then the goddess asked me that from which town did I come? But before I replied to her question, I first sat on one of the diamond chairs which were in that court. I replied that I come from my village which was about six days' journey to the sea. She asked that on which road did I travel to her town? I replied that I did not purposely come to her town but when my canoe was capsized by the strong wave and wind, then I was brought to the shore and from there one of her camels brought me to her town. She asked again that what was I finding about, a young man like me. But I replied that I was finding the treasures about to take to my village. I told her further that I was very happy to come to her town that time because I had seen plenty of diamonds in her court which I would take to my village.

But she hardly heard like that when sneered at me greatly and with anger, she remarked: "I wonder, why every human being never satisfy with whatever his Creator had provided for him!" But I replied: "That was how our Creator had created all human beings." Then she said: "You are a robber then if you are finding the treasures about. But you cannot take any of my diamonds to your village. And it is doubtful if you can leave this town again!" Having said like that she told her men to take me to the guardroom to lock me up there. Without hesitation, I was escorted to that room and I was locked up. The guardroom was opposite her court and by that I could see everything clearly. But of course, one who was locked up in that room was going to die soon. Because she never allowed anybody to come to her town so that her diamonds might not be stolen.

As I was in that room, I noticed that every seat and the decorations in that court were diamonds. Both the walls and the floor were shining. All were so shining that I had to guide my eyes with palm before I saw anything. In another room which opposite that court had no door at all and there were three standing figures of men and three standing figures of women. All were made of diamonds and also the diamond blocks in it were uncountable. The Goddess of Diamonds herself was just like the diamonds because she was so dressed in diamonds that she had nearly to turn into the diamonds. Of course, she was old and was unable to walk about so much. The uniforms of her attendants were almost made with diamonds. She and the rest people of her town worshipped that standing figures of men and women. It were their gods.

It was so I was thinking how to steal some of the diamonds to my village as I was in the guardroom. Then when it was about seven o'clock in the evening, the goddess went to her rest room which was quite far from there and after a while all her attendants left there as well. Then it remained me alone in that guardroom. But as I was still thinking how to come out of that room, one young beautiful lady came to me, she was one of the attendants. She stood behind the door and then stretched right hand to me and she began to caress me. She asked about my village and I told her. After a while she started to amuse me until when my fear was expelled. But when she noticed that I began to answer all her questions with fearless voice. Then she told me that she was the very lady who had been sending the bananas, plantains, yams, fresh water, etc. to me when I was at the bottom of the mountain. She said that she had seen me since when my canoe had broken into pieces and that when the wave had carried me to the shore. She said that her name was Sela and that she was next to the senior attendant.

While she was still talking to me, when the senior attendant was coming to the court, then she left me as hastily as possible. In the following morning, this beautiful lady, Sela, wrapped a nice food, hid it under her dress and brought it to me and I thanked her greatly as she was returning to the court as quickly as possible so that the other attendants might not suspect her. But as soon as I understood through her free will and the interest she had in me and which proved that she liked me whole-heartedly, therefore, I was always talking to her cheerfully whenever she came to me. I wondered greatly to meet this kind of a lady in this remote place although their race was quite different from my own. Because she was so kind to me that each time she visited me, she brought wrapped food to me which I was eating. And I was saved through her help because the goddess did not bother whether I ate or not.

One day, I told her with fear and trembling voice that I should be happy if she would let me marry her. I thought she would not agree or to become annoy with me. But as she was already expecting to hear this from me. So she agreed with pleasure at the same time, but she explained that it was impossible for me to marry her and then stay in that town for the goddess was going to kill me soon as a trespasser because many people whose canoes had sunk in the sea had come to that town for help but the goddess had killed all of them.

Having spent about five months in the guardroom, one morning, I was brought before the goddess in her court to try my case. But as she tried so many cases that morning, so she postponed my own for one month. But of course, I had no rest of mind since when that lady had hinted me that the penalty for a trespasser like me was death. So one midnight, when she brought wrapped food to me, I told her to be get ready to let us escape from that town to my village in the following midnight and she agreed. This was very risky because the goddess had never allowed any of her attendants to marry to any man and she had never allowed any of them to go out of that town.

Anyhow, before that night, she had packed plenty of diamonds in a big bag and kept it in a deep pit. She tied one healthy and fast-moving camel, to one tree which was near that pit. So when it was twelve o'clock of the following night, Sela woke up from her room, having noticed well that there was nobody woke that time, she came to me cautiously. She opened the door of the guardroom and I came out. I went to the room in which the diamond blocks were kept. I put one block in my hunting-bag and after that I broke the head of one of the diamond figures of men which were also kept in that room and were worshipped by the goddess and her people. I tied it up with a rope and hung it on my shoulder together with my gun, hunting-bag and matchet. After that Sela took one lamp which was hung near the entrance of the court.

Then both of us walked cautiously to that pit. We took the heavy bag out and tied it to the back of that camel and my gun and hunting-bag, which was also full of diamonds, were tied to the back of the camel as well. But my matchet and the rest diamonds were on my shoulder. After that we mounted that camel. Sela who knew the road, sat in the front holding that lamp and I sat at the back nearly to touch her. Then we rode to the outside of the town.

Having travelled a short distance to the town, we stopped and the lamp was lit up because there was dark. She hung it on the neck of the camel and it was shining to the front. After that we kept galloping down the mountain. We did all these things so cautiously that none of the rest people woke from sleep. But we were unable to travel so far when it was the dawn, because of the rocks, holes, big fallen trees, etc., all these things were great hinderances to our travel. We were unable to travel as fast as we had wanted to.

When it was about three o'clock a.m. we left the top of the mountain and we began to descend. It was so steep that we were rolling with the camel to a short distance several times in a few minutes. As we were disturbing by the deep pits, it was so we were disturbing by the big fallen trees and rocks. And it was so we were disturbing as well by the wild animals like lions, wolves, tigers, etc. and the snakes of all kinds. But with bravery, we were still galloping down the mountain as fast as the camel could.

After a while, when the troubles were too much for us, I began to blame myself that if I had known that to descend the mountain was so dangerous and troublesome like this, I should had not attempted to leave that town at all but to surrender myself to the Goddess of Diamonds to be killed. As I was still blaming myself, several lions, tigers and wolves were rushing to us from every part of the mountain to kill us. Having seen them in that fearful attitudes, then I took my gun and I began to shoot those wolves to death so that we might be freed from the lions and tigers when they ate their bodies. Luckily, when they ate some of them and were satisfied, they left us and went away.

But as we were just freed from that wild animals, and we were still descending the mountain. There we heard a horrible shout from the top of the mountain. When we looked at the top very far off, we saw the goddess on the steeple of the tower which was in her town. As she stood on it, and as we were still within her sight, she shouted greatly: "Bring Sela back to me now! Bring my diamonds back to me now!" But we did not go back to her. And as we continued to gallop down and down, she shouted very terribly again: "If you don't bring Sela back to me now, I shall send my men soon to bring her back but put in mind that the day I shall send my men to your village will be very bad and unfortunate to you and your people as well!"

When she warned me like that and was still squabbling repeatedly, I feared so much that I wanted to leave Sela and then run away for my life. But she told me not to pay heed to her. When it was about three o'clock p.m., we came to the sea and then we came down from the camel. Having put our loads down, we ate because we had had no time to wait and eat since when we had left that town in the night. And having given food to the camel and we waited for about two hours. Luckily, one big canoe was passing this time. We waved hands to the paddlers and the canoe was paddled to us.

After we put our loads in it and we went in it, then the paddlers continued to paddle it along. But that camel was waiting on the shore until it saw us no more and then it began to return to the town of the Goddess of Diamonds. After a few days' travel, we came to my village at about seven o'clock in the evening. Then I went direct to my father's house with the lady, Sela, and the diamonds.

It was not so long when the people of my village knew that I had brought one beautiful lady from my fifth journey when they rushed to my father's house, to perform the marriage ceremony together with my father and mother. The old men of my father's age first prayed and then my father advised my wife thus: "I advise you to be 'a stagnant' wife and not 'a flowing away' wife. A 'flowing away' wife always flowing away like the stream of water when it is hard for her husband. Always flowing away when her husband is in difficulties. A 'flowing away' wife is flowing away when her husband is in sickness and on death-bed. Bad wife never drink the bitter tea with her husband except the sweet tea. Bad wife always departs from her husband when he is hard up but she pretends to be a good wife when her husband is well to do. But 'a stagnant' wife always remains whole-heartedly when it is hard for her husband. She never departs when her husband is in troubles or in difficulties. She shares from her husband's bitterness and not comfort alone." Then he (my father) turned to me and advised me thus: "Yes, you are my son! When it is time for a son to have his own 'bow and arrow' he should have them without delay! So it is time for you to have a wife and you have it today! But be a good husband to your wife A good husband does not pay heed to all his wife's mistakes, wrong doings, etc., otherwise he will come back to a redundant bachelor or a redundant husband!" Then after my father had advised both of us, my wife Sela, knelt and thanked him greatly. It was like that Sela became my wife that day and the people shouted with joy and then the merriments began till the late hour of the night.

According to the custom, I killed many rams and he-goats which when were cooked were served with the drinks as the merriment was still going on.

After a few months, Sela proved to be a good wife, so my people and all the people of the village liked her so much that they were taking great care of her and were giving presents to her whenever I went to another village for a few days.

Having sold all the diamonds which I had brought from the town of the Goddess of Diamonds, I had enough money and having built a very beautiful storey which had many flats, then I resigned to go to any journey again, but several young men of the village were advising me always to continue the journey so that they might follow me, of course, I did not pay heed to their advice at all for I was satisfied with all I had that time.

"Now, my people, I thank you greatly for listening to the story of my fifth journey. The entertainment of the journey is not finished yet but as the night is becoming too cold and the moon is becoming deem, so I shall continue to tell you the rest story tomorrow night. Good night, everybody!"

Then my people drank the rest of their palm-wine and having danced and sung for a few minutes then they shouted with great joy and then went back to their houses.

The Day of Separation from My Wife

The entertainment of the seventh night

It was hardly eight o'clock of the seventh night when the people of my village had gathered in front of my house. All sat quietly as usual and were waiting to hear the rest part of my fifth journey. But as soon as the palm-wine was served to every one of them and the biggest keg was in front of me and as I was enjoying it with my pipe. I sat up in my usual old arm-chair and then the entertainment began as follows:

Now, listen well, my people! But it is a great pity to tell you that in those days. As I was living comfortably with my father, mother, sister, brother and my wife, Sela, in my new storey building. So in the early morning that I completed one year that I had brought Sela to the village, a terrible thing happened, which I had not experienced in my life although I had been to several risky and dangerous towns, villages, forests, jungles and I had been changed into the image for a number of years but this was too terrible to me. It was terrible indeed to the people, animals and trees of the village.

It was hardly four o'clock of the morning when there were signs all over the village and its surroundings. As I lay on the bed together with my wife and were still enjoying the sleep of that morning. There I woke suddenly by all kinds of powerful and terrible noises. My bed was shaking, the cloth on my body was biting my body and it was so all the walls and roof were shaking as if they were going to fall down very soon.

Having seen this, and as the cloth on my body was biting every part of my body, I did not know when I threw it away from my body and I ran to the door to open it and then to peep out and see what was happening at the outside. But the door was so shaking with all its power that I could not touch it with hands. Having seen this again, I hastily left it and ran to the lamp with great fear and trembling body. But I hardly touched it just to light it up when it flung itself far away and then fell down with great noise. Again, without hesitation, I left there with fear and then I ran in to my father's room. But as it was shaking very terribly as well, I ran out from there with fear and then I ran in back to my own room. But as the shakes were still increasing, I was unable to hesitate but I rushed out to the door of the premises and I forced it open and I hastily jumped out as it was still making great noise and shaking terribly.

And I hardly jumped to the outside when I began to stagger along in the village. Again, I saw that all trees of the village were shaking terribly, the ground was shaking as if it was going to sink in that moment. The domestic animals were shaking and staggering about in the village. But to my fear again, as I was still staggering along with perplexity, with the hope to hide in anywhere that I might see perhaps that would save me. Unfortunately I saw thousands of people who were staggering about in the village in search for somewhere in which to hide themselves as well. All of them were driving away from their houses by the same thing which was driving me about.

I was so feared this morning that I did not remember to cover my body. Now, neither the people nor the domestic animals could stay in the village or in the bush. The whole of us were rushing here and there in the village and were dashing to each other several times with fear and embarrassment.

At last, when it was about six o'clock in the morning, these strange fearful happenings came to the climax. The shakes and the terrible noises of the invisible people were increasing alarmingly. This time we were despaired and we had lost all our hope. Because after a while the thunder and lightning began to roar continuously. When this was too much for us to bear, then everyone began to shout for help. The dumps who could not speak were murmuring, the deafs raised heads up to their Creator and were expecting help from Him although they could not hear. And with great fear, the cocks crowed, the elephants trumpeted, the lames crept, the dogs barked, the horses neighed, the cats jumped, the goats butted the ewes, the rams scratched the ground to escape into it, the bats scattered all over the sky with fear.

And, willing or not, irons dropped juice by force but yet all these things did not stop. When the thunder was so roaring terribly with lightning that the people could no longer stand or remain at outside, then I staggered back to my house. I lay on the bed with my wife, we held the bed as it was shaking as if it was going to turn upside. And it was not so long when we were holding it when it threw us on to the floor so heavily that some of my ribs were fractured and my wife was fractured on the left thigh. So when we stood up at the same time we walked zigzag back to the bed like a crab, and then both of us pretended to be asleep with fear, but it was impossible.

Again, when we could not stay on the bed any longer, I jumped down and my wife hastily did the same thing. Then I ran to the main door, I forced it open and I jumped to the outside again with my wife, father, mother, brother and sister. Then we continued to hurtle to everywhere in the village with the rest people. As we were still hurtling about with fear and restlessness of minds, these terrible things stopped suddenly. Then everyone went back to his or her house. In that moment, there was no noise again, everything became quiet at the same time but the quietness was fearful as well. Because the breeze stopped entirely to blow, all of the trees stood still and all of the domestic animals stood still as well and they did not mind to escape if one came to kill them that moment. Not knowing that all these had happened in respect of my wife, Sela. All happenings were the signs that she was taking back to the Goddess of Diamonds by her men whom she sent.

As we were still wondering at the sudden quietness, there we saw that the thick forg covered the whole village suddenly and we were unable to see ourselves. This forg was so thick that if two persons stood closely to each other, one could not see the second. After a while, as my wife and I peeped from the door and we were thinking of the place to escape to, then this forg gathered into one place under the tree in front of my house. And without hesitation, two strong men appeared immediately the forg disappeared. One of the men was on camel and he was a very strong archer. He held the shield of silver which contained many diamond ornaments. His bow was thick and long. He shielded himself from legs to the neck with ornamented silver. He wore the silver shoes and covered both wrists to the shoulders with diamonds. The hat on his head was high and was full of several skulls of the sea animals and several skulls of the sea fish were tacked to it as well. The front of this hat formed a fearful mask over his face, so his eyes could not be seen to be described.

The second one was on horse, he was older than the first one who was on camel. He armoured himself from the waist to the neck with a thick leather. The ornaments on it were lizards, crocodiles, alligators, heads of sharks, lobsters, etc. He shielded both legs with a rough thick leather of whale and his shoes were silver. The hat on his head had four heads, each represented a kind of wild animal and all faced different direction. The first one which faced frontward was the head of a lion, the second which faced the east was the head of a deer which had several branched horns. The third one which faced the west was the head of a boa constrictor and the fourth one which faced the south, was the head of a tiger. All these heads were seemed as if they were alive and all were on top of his hat, so by that the top of it was flat and round like a tray. He held a heavy cudgel of diamond. He was very very fearful to see, therefore, I was unable to look at the rest part of his body.

But as I was still recollecting these two men were resembled the gods of the Goddess of Diamonds and again I noticed that my wife shrank up that moment when she saw them, then I believed at the same time that the men were sent by the Goddess of Diamonds. But of course, the Goddess of Diamonds had told me that it would be bad for me and for the people, etc. of my village the day she sent her men to bring Sela back to her and it was true at last. Now, when I remembered that these two men were the men of the Goddess of Diamonds and my wife, Sela, knew them too as the men of her mother. So as we were about to rush in and shut the door. The fearful men looked upon her suddenly, but as they shouted: "Ah, this is Sela (waving hands to her)! Come and let us go!" Then both of us rushed in and I hastily slammed the door. Then we went direct to the top floor and we peeped through one of the windows and then we were looking at them.

But when they raised heads up and saw us, they began to wave hands to Sela to come down to them. When she refused to come down, one who was the strong archer began to shoot the arrows to us. Having seen this, we shut that window and we escaped into the room. At last, when they failed to get hold of my wife, then one of them shouted greatly with a kind of a voice. And within a few seconds, a heavy rain together with wind came. As it was raining and everything was then blowing here and there by the wind then we saw a powerful lightning which was coming down from the sky and without hesitation, it broke the window and then entered the house.

And as we were running with fear and embarrassment from one room to the other just to escape the lightning, the whole house caught fire and it was so strong that its flame was burning everything in the house at the same time. As my wife and I and also my people were running here and there with great embarrassment just to escape, the two men began to ride round the house and were watching when the fire would drive us down to them.

At last, when we were nearly burnt with the house and some parts of our dresses had already caught fire, then I shouted greatly for help. Within a few moments, several people came out with ladders and they hastily stretched the longest one on the wall of the back of the house. But before the people came to rescue us, the two men had hidden themselves in somewhere near the house. So my father, mother, sister, brother, my wife and I came down by that ladder as hastily as we could because the roof was falling down repeatedly by that time.

But we hardly stepped down from the ladder when these two men rushed out from their hiding place. But immediately the people who had come to rescue us saw these two fearful men, they were afraid and then ran back to their houses because they had never seen the kind of these men before.

As they rushed to us, then one held my wife and the second one put one kind of a diamond hat on her head. After that both of them lifted the whole of her from the ground on to the horse. But as they were about to ride away, I hastily snatched her from the horse. And as she fell from the horse on to the ground and then I was pulling her up just to take her away. One who was holding the cudgel of diamond, rushed to me and then struck my left shoulder so heavily that I fell down helplessly within that moment. Then without hesitation he snatched her back from me and he put her back on the horse and they began to ride along before I got up. Having seen this, I shouted to the people again for help. Then they rushed out in great number. Some held cudgels, some held bows and arrows and some held cutlasses. Then we were chasing them along in the village.

After a while, we overtook them, but as some of us were just snatching my wife from the horse, these two men began to shoot the bow to us. Having seen this, my people began to shoot their bows to them in return. After a while, it turned to a serious war. As we were shooting them and beating them with cudgels it was so they too were beating us with their cudgel of diamond and shooting their bows to us repeatedly. We tried all our efforts to take my wife back from them but all were in vain. At last, when they overpowered us, then they rode furiously away with my wife. It was like that my wife, Sela, who had saved me from the prison of the Goddess of Diamonds, was taken back to her mother.

Then we came back to my house and the people helped me to quench that fire, but it was too late, all my property had burnt into ashes. It was like that all the treasures which I had brought from all my journeys had gone away. But when there was nothing remained with me then I thought over to continue my journey, perhaps I might be as rich as before although I had promised not to go any journey since when I had returned from my fifth journey.

Then the people of my village wondered greatly when they heard this story of my fifth journey. After they drank, sang and danced with joy for some minutes then they went back to their houses when the moon was becoming dark.

The Foot Marks of the First White Men who had travelled from Heaven to the World were seen on the Rock in Ife Town. And we visited the Wells from which the Sun and Moon are rising into the Sky and we met the God of Thunder and his Wife in Ede Town

The entertainment of the eighth night

(*My sixth Journey*)

And it was hardly nine o'clock of the eighth night, as the moon was just appeared, when the whole people of my village had gathered in front of my house. When all of them sat quietly then everyone was served with one keg of the palm-wine and the biggest keg was in front of me. After they had drunken some of their wine and then sung and danced for a while, and when I put the fire in my pipe and then sat up in my usual old arm-chair. Then when the people sat back quietly and were ready to hear my story. I began to tell them the story of my sixth journey thus:

Although I had discontinued my journeys since when I had brought Sela to the village from her mother, the Goddess of Diamonds, the ruler of the town on the mountain. But of course, since when she had been taken away and again, all of my property had burnt into ashes. Therefore, I made up my mind to continue my journeys once more, probably I might be a rich man as before, after the journeys.

But as I was just preparing to leave in a few days' time for another town in which there were treasures as beads, raw gold, silver, brass, copper, etc. in which the inhabitants of that town were not interested. So six of my friends insisted to go with me. They told me that they too liked to be rich when they returned. Of course, I told them the difficulties, dangers, punishments, starvation of the roads, etc. But yet, they insisted to go with me, then I allowed them to follow me, for I believed that soon or later they would understand that all the wealths which I had brought to the village and had been burnt into the ashes, had not been stolen nor had I been monopolized people of their properties, but I had done a lot of dangerous and risky works for them before they had given them to me as rewards.

Now, in the morning that I was leaving, I borrowed one gun, because my own gun had burnt the other day. Then I put some edible things in the new hunting-bag which I hung on my left shoulder together with the gun. Then I held my usual matchet, after that I bade my father, mother, etc. good-bye. I hardly done that when my six friends came, then we left the village at the same time. But the town in which I was going this time was under the ground and the entrance of it was invisible and before we could trace it out, we would travel as far as to Ile-Ife. And it was in Ife town the sun and the moon were rising from different wells into the sky and were setting in the same wells. Of course I was very happy as I was talking and joking with my friends along the road, I was not lonely at all as my last five journeys. (ILE-IFE is in the West of Nigeria.)

Having travelled for many weeks, with much difficulties, etc. we reached Ife town at about six o'clock in the evening. But it took us some hours again to reach the "boundary keeper's lodge" because we were attracted by the wonders which we saw on the way leading to his lodge. And we were very lucky that there was no darkness in Ife town because it was from there the sun and the moon rised and set. Therefore, everything was very clear to us through the rays of the moon.

After a while, we met one of the inhabitants of Ife on the

road and as we did not know the way to the "boundary man's lodge" or porter's lodge. So he led us to the lodge which was at the outskirt of the town. We reached there at about ten o'clock in the night. But he was not in that moment, he had gone to the town, of course one of his attendants was sent to him to inform him of our arrival. After a few minutes, he returned with his attendant. He entered his sitting-room and when he sat, we were invited to come in and then we prostrated and saluted him with great respect. Having answered us with a cheerful voice, then he ordered us to stand from the prostration otherwise we must not stand up, or if we did so it was an insult to him. So we sat before him.

Then he asked from us: "My sons, from where did you come?" I hastily knelt before him and replied: "We come from a village in Abeokuta." He said at the same time: "Oh, is that so? Good! But what did you come to me for?" I replied: "We come to you to show us the invisible entrance to the town which is under the ground." But he laughed greatly when he heard like that from me. He was so much surprised that he repeated the name of that town several times within that moment. But with bravery, I still confirmed that we were going to the town which was under the ground.

Then he explained to us as the old men of my village had already explained, that the inhabitants of that town were very dangerous. But when I told him that I had already heard about that, he shrugged and then said that he would show us the entrance later on. He said that we must spend a few days with him so that he might take us round Ife town to see the wonders and also the king of Ife who was the father of all Yorubas.

After a while he told his servant to give us food and drink and having eaten and drunken, then we played for a while before we were taken to the bedroom and then we slept.

When we woke up in the morning, we met him (porter) in

the sitting-room. He sat on his old ornamented arm-chair and he was chewing stick while the hot drink was in front of him. We prostrated flatly before him and saluted him according to how young Yoruba men were saluting an old and high rank man as he was. He answered cheerfully and then he first gave one shot of that hot drink to each of us. Then he gave chewing sticks to us and having chewed it then we went to the bathroom to bathe. But the morning pap was ready before we returned from the bathroom and it was served hot to each of us as soon as we returned.

After the pap, and he amused us for a while, then he stood up and as he was leaving the sitting-room, he told us to follow him. First, he took us to the well from which the moon was rising into the sky. When we peeped into this well, the water reached a half of it and it was very clear. The well had no bottom at all. And we saw the moon in it as it was moving round like a wheel. It shone to every part of the well as if it was as big as the sky. But of course, we were unable to look at it so long for its ray was too powerful for the eyes. Having left the moon, he took us to one vast rock which went along without end. When we climbed it to the distance of about one half of a mile. Then we came to where several foot marks were appeared on this rock. Some went up that rock and so some went down. He showed us two foot marks which proved that one who had walked on there had shoes on feet and both went downward as if one who had the marks had descended from the rock. When I asked the porter why those two were quite different from the rest, he told us that those foot marks which bore the shoe marks, were belonged to the first white men who had first travelled from heaven through that rock to the earth.

Again, he showed us the road leading to heaven but it was very rough indeed and full of refuses. But when I asked him why that road was so rough and full of refuses while the others were very clean, he explained to us that because the people hated to go back to heaven always. But as he had omitted one thing in which I had much interest. So I asked him to show us the well from which the sun was rising into the sky. He replied without delay that as that time was the day-time and that the sun was on, we could not go near it or if we did so, we would burn into the ashes at the same moment. Of course, he pointed finger to the well and in fact nobody could go near it in the day-time because we saw plainly the heat which was rushing out of the well. He told us further that all the people of Ife town did not worry to go to another town for fire but they were getting their fire from the heat of the sun.

After that he took us to the palace of Oduduwa, the father of all Yorubas, and we met his successor in his (Oduduwa's) robes. And with happiness, the king took us round the palace and we saw many images, gods, idols, etc. which he and his royal family were worshipped. After we returned to the palace and sat in front of him and his chiefs. Then he started to explain to us that all Yoruba Obas (kings) like the Alake of Abeokuta, Alafin of Oyo, Owa of Ilesha, Alaketu of Dahomey, Olubini of Benin, etc. etc. etc., were the sons of Oduduwa. Again, I told him to show us the grave of Oduduwa. But to my surprise, he and his chiefs and the porter bursted into a great laughter at a time. Then the king explained that Oduduwa did not die at all but he walked from the earth back to heaven when he was old and weary. But when he noticed that we did not believe him, he, together with his chiefs and the porter, took us to the road on which Oduduwa had travelled back to the heaven in those days. To everyone's astonishment, there was no bush or weed sprouted on that road since when he had travelled on it. But it was as clear as if somebody was sweeping it every moment and so it is till today.

We remained in the palace till the following morning. We ate and drank as we liked. The king and his chiefs advised us very strongly not to go to that town which was under the ground, but I refused. So when it was about nine o'clock we followed the porter back to his lodge after the king and his chiefs had given us many presents.

In the following morning which was the third day that we had arrived in Ife town. The porter took us to another town which was called Ede, the home of the god of thunder and his wife whose name was Oya. But we travelled for two days before we came to Ede town. Then the porter took us direct to the palace of the god of thunder. Luckily we met him and his wife, Oya, in their respective robes with which they worshipped their gods. When the porter introduced us to him and told him the kind of persons we were, he and his wife shook hands with every one of us. After a while, we were served with nice food and drinks of all kinds. After we ate and drank, then he and his wife took us to his gods which were occupied the whole of a mighty building. This building was far away from the palace or any other buildings because the gods in it were so powerful that people could not live near them.

As he stood before his gods, just to show us how powerful they (gods) were, he took one big gourd which was hung before them. The shape of that gourd was just like that of bottle of beer. Some round pebbles were put in it before it was cocked. Its outer part was entirely soaked with the blood of the animals which had been sacrificed to the gods and plenty of cock's and hen's feathers were stuck to every part of it. Then he started to shake this gourd as hastily as he could as he was talking to it.

To our fear this day was that, he hardly shook it for about thirty seconds when the sky became very cloudy, and a few seconds more, a heavy rain came but immediately the rain began, we saw his wife who stood before her own gods as well in another part of that building. And she took her own gourd which was a little different from her husband's. She held it with right hand and she took one thick copper (about one foot long) from the mud bowl which was before the gods. The head of that copper had two thick edges. Each of the edges was in shape of axe but much shorter. As she was shaking the gourd with the right hand and held up that copper with the left hand and as her husband was still shaking his own continuously. Then there was lightning and thunder. As the lightning was flashing into this building with great power and as several thunderbolts were dashing in repeatedly, it was so she was snatching them with the copper which was in her left hand and then she was dropping them in the mud bowl which was in front of her gods. (Songo is male, the god of thunder, and Oya is female. So when the god of thunder vexes, his wife, Oya, appeases him with the copper.)

As the husband was shaking the gourd continuously with great anger and the thunderbolts were dashing in and the lightning was flashing in with full force but when his wife caught the thunderbolts for some minutes then he hung his gourd back before his gods and then the thunderbolts and the lightning were stopped at the same time and the rain stopped after a while as well. After everything was stopped, then Oya hung her own gourd back before her own gods as well.

It was like that we had enjoyed their displays. Then we went back to the palace after more wonders had been shown to us. But when we got ready to leave in the following morning, the husband (god of thunder) gave us four black tablets which, when swallowed, would turn us into another form. His wife, Oya, gave us four red tablets as well which, when swallowed, would change us back to our former forms whenever we turned into anything. Then we thanked them greatly before we left their town.

The entertainment of the eighth night

We reached Ife town in the third day. But as we did not want to keep long there again, so I told the porter in the night that we would continue our journey in the following morning. He told us to wait and enjoy more days with him but I told him that we were anxious greatly to reach where we were going as early as possible. So he agreed and then prayed for us that we would reach our destination savely and that we would return to our village savely as well.

The Hairy Giant and the Hairy Giantess

The entertainment of the ninth night

The people of my village were gathered earlier in the front of my house to hear the continuation story of my sixth journey. All were served with the palm-wine as usual and then I continued to tell the story as follows:

In the following morning, when we were ready to leave, the porter or the boundary-keeper asked us to show him the weapons with which we were travelling. But when I showed him my gun and machet and my friends showed him their own matchets as well, he bursted into a great laughter. He told us that all our weapons cannot save us from the dangers of the underground, especially the fearful hairy giant and the hairy giantess whom we were going to meet on the way. But of course, as he was a kind porter, he gave us plenty of bows and poisonous arrows. After that we told him to show us the invisible road which led into the underground. So he pointed hand to a kind of a house which was far away but within our sights.

This house, as I called it, was as narrow and long as a chimney. It showed that it had been built with mud more than two hundred years. Its narrow entrance was very rough and the withered leaves were full up the bottom of it and this showed that people were not going through there to the underground town frequently. It was closed with a very heavy flat stone which about one hundred men could not move. There was a small space on top of it through which something like smoke was rushing straight into the sky.

We felt very reluctant when the porter told us to go to this house and bow down for three times before we knock at the stone which was the door for the entrance. Anyhow, after we had thanked him greatly for his kindness and then bade good-bye to him and his family, we started to go to this house with doubtful minds. Having travelled hastily for thirty minutes we came to the house and then all of us stood before its entrance. Having bowed down for three times, then I knocked and we were waiting for the reply. After a while, we saw many hands which pushed that heavy stone to one side and then we heard a weary voice which told us to come in. But to our surprise, we did not see the rest bodies of the owners of those hands and we did not see the person who had told us to come in as well.

Anyhow, with bravery, I entered the house and my friends followed me with fear. Immediately I entered and walked to a short distance, I saw a long ladder which went into the underground. Then I began to climb that ladder down as my friends were following me. When we climbed it for about one hour then we came to the ground of the underground. But as we stood in one place and were still wondering to see that this underground was another world, one middle-aged man, who was completely in black dress, came to us. He told us that we were wanted. When he said so, I asked him with a soft voice: "We are wanted by whom?" He replied: "By my father who is the keeper of this place!" Then we followed him with the hope that his father was near that place. But after we had travelled with him for about two hours, we came to a very high rock and without hesitation, we were following him as he was climbing that rock along to the top.

When we got to the top, we saw his father sitting on an old wooden chair. Having brought us to his father and as we bowed and were saluting him, this middle-aged man entered the house which was behind his father. After the salutation, the father told us to sit before him and each of us sat on each of the stones which were at a little distance in front of him like the visitors' seats. I hardly sat down when I began to notice his appearances and surroundings. He was so old that he seemed that he could not die. He was old beyond death. Because all the muscle of his body had already dried up to the state that when he stood up there was no difference between him and a dried slender stick. Neither of his eyes had dried up to the size of a bean. His cheeks had already melted but his teeth were complete. His legs were stretched forward as if both could not move to anywhere. But what made us afraid was that the hairs on his head were very few but his beard was long up to ten feet and all went along on the ground. One guana lay down on his left and one snail on his right. The snail was as big as a load which a strong man could not even move to one side. Of course, I could not say the kind of helps that which the guana and the snail were rendering to him.

But as I began to notice his surroundings, he asked suddenly: "I believe, you were the persons who had knocked at the door of the entrance!" When I replied: "Yes," he asked again: "Where are you going?" I replied: "We are going to the town of wealths!" "What for?" he asked. I replied: "We are going there for wealths!" "Wealths?" he repeated it with great wonder and I confirmed it loudly: "Yes, indeed!"

Then he looked at the sky and thought over for a few minutes before he raised head down and told us that he was very sorry that the hairy giant and hairy giantess who were on the rock would kill us as soon as we climbed that rock to the top. Having told us like that I asked him whether there was another road on which to travel but he said that there was only one road in the underground. When he told us like that some of us were so much feared that they wanted to return to the village from there. But this old man hastily explained to us that we could not go back again because once we had entered the underground, there was no way to go back except to go forward.

Then all of us became quiet at the same time, we did not talk until the old man asked whether we knew him before, but I said: "We did not know you before because we had not come into the underground before." After that he explained to us that he was there as well to be interviewing those who were coming in to the underground. He said that every newcomer was bound to pay the boundary fee to him before he or she would be allowed to proceed on his or her journey.

Then I asked him for how much we were going to pay, but he told us that it was ten thousand cowries (about threepence) per head. Then I gave him seven threepences from the money which was given to us by the king of Ife town and the king of Ede town, the god of thunder. These seven threepences were the boundary fees for the whole of us. After the payment, he stood up like the skeleton and then he blessed every one of us before he allowed us to go. But we could not travel so far when it was night. Then we slept under one tree which was on a small hill near the road and we woke up in the morning and then continued to travel along as early as possible.

We felt to eat when we had travelled as hastily as we could till twelve o'clock. Then we stopped under one of the mango trees which lined up along the road on which were travelling. We hesitated for some minutes perhaps we would see the owner of these fruit trees so that we might beg him to give us some of the fruits. Having hesitated for a while but we did not see anyone. Then one of us, whose name was Ajasa, climbed one of the trees. As he was plucking the ripen mangoes down to us and we were eating them with greediness and as he was eating them on top of that tree. One fearful man and his wife appeared from a distance of about five hundred yards.

Then the whole of us stopped eating the mangoes at the same time but we gazed at both of them as they were coming direct to that place. When they came nearer, we saw them clearly that the man was a giant and his wife was a giantess. None of them wore clothes but their bodies were full of hair. The hair were as fluffy as that of a cat but had many spots like that of a leopard. The hair of their heads were very bushy and made the heads bigger and so the hair of their feet were bushy and made the feet bigger as if they wore shoes. Their palms had no hair at all but their mouths were hardly to see when were shut up because of the hair which made them seemed as if there were no mouths at all. But of course, their eyes were seen always because of the eyeballs which were swelled out like a big knob of a big tree.

Their nose were very big and the nostrils were full of hair. Each of their teeth was about a half of an inch wide and about two inches long. The husband was about twelve feet tall and was very stout and strong and smart. Both of them were always seemed as if they were in a great anger. But I noticed again that the eyeballs of his wife were four times bigger than the husbands. She had the breasts which were nearly to touch the ground.

The husband held one short thick cudgel of stone and it was so heavy that he placed it on the shoulder as he held it. His wife held one dead antelope with the left hand and one half-dead hawk with the right hand. Immediately both of them saw us, the husband held his cudgel of stone very tightly and then raised it above head this time.

But when they were about twenty yards from us, the husband shouted greatly: "Who are you? Who are you eating my mangoes? Stop in one place and let your death meets you there or be running away and let your death chase you! Please, choose neither of the two! Because I am the death who is coming to kill you all now! Willing or not all of you will go in my soup pot tonight!" But when this fearful hairy giant shouted like that and was getting ready to beat us with his cudgel of stone as both were coming to us with great anger. So without hesitation, we snatched our loads from the ground and then we started to run along on the road for our lives. But unfortunately Ajasa, who was on top of that mango tree, was unable to climb down and follow us, until the hairy giant came to the tree and then threw his cudgel of stone to him as that was still trembling with fear. But when the cudgel missed him but was hung between two branches. Having failed to bring Ajasa down with his cudgel he began to climb the tree to the top as hastily as he could just to take it and then to beat him to death at the same time.

Having seen him coming up to him, Ajas hastily jumped from the top of that mango tree to another one which was nearby. But as this fearful hairy giant was still struggling hardly to take his cudgel in time and then to jump from that mango tree on to the second one on which Ajasa was and as his wife, the hairy giantess, was going round that tree so that Ajasa might not be able to jump down before her husband would be able to come to him. Ajasa jumped on to another part of the ground suddenly and without hesitation, he was running away as fast as he could.

When the giant had taken his cudgel and come down from the mango tree, he and his wife started to chase us. After a while, Ajasa overtook us, and then we were running along together as fast we we could. After a while we were lost within the sight of the giant and his wife. But of course, that was not so long when we ran to one hill on top of which the road went along to the other side. Then without hesitation, and as we were breathing in and out heavily for tiredness, we began to climb it with all our power. And with much difficulties and tiredness, we climbed it to the top when it was about six o'clock in the evening.

As we were very tired before climbing this hill to the top and as the darkness of the night was coming gradually. So we did not waste time but we began to find a place in which to hide ourselves at the same time before the hairy giant and giantess came. As there were some houses on top of the hill which had already ruined from a long time. Therefore it was very hard for us to find a hiding place as soon as possible. The roofs of these houses had already fallen down and the walls were badly split and some were nearly washed away by the rains. So this showed us that the inhabitants had left there or died from a long time. But there were many fowls, goats, rams, etc. which were seeing everywhere in this ruined town.

But as we were trying to hide ourselves before this fearful man and his wife came. So without hesitation, we entered one of these ruined houses but we hardly entered when the fowls which were perched on the walls and beams scattered and began to make great noise. Then without hesitation, we ran out so that they might not suspect us to the giant. Again, we ran to another one which was next to that and without hesitation, we entered it but we ran out with fear when several big and small birds which were perched in there to sleep scattered by that time. Again, without hesitation, we ran to another one but as there was no shelter on the floor of it we began to climb it so that we might hide on some of the beams which were not yet fallen down. But as we sat on the beams and then we were peeping and expecting when the giant and his wife would come, the beams together with the old walls fell down suddenly and all were broken into pieces. And all of us were wounded but two of us were wounded seriously and they were fainted before we took them out from the fallen walls and beams.

Having taken them out, I hastily cut some long strips from the stem of the plantains which was near there Then I used them as bandages for the wounded parts of the bodies of those two men. After that I cut some palm-fronds and wove them. So we carried these two men with them to another house as hastily as possible. But this house was not so ruined and it showed that somebody was living in it. Because I noticed that there were pots of water, plates, brooms, one big mortar and pestle, soup pots and a very big hearth in which there was a big fire, was in the centre of the house. All these things were not in order at all and this showed us that the person who was living in there was not so normal.

Anyhow, we did not think so much about the owner before we entered one of the four rooms. We lay the two wounded men near left corner and then the rest of us lay in the second corner which was on the right. But as we were very tired, so it was not long when we fell asleep without putting our loads and gun inside, all were in the front of that house. Not knowing that this house belonged to the fearful hairy giant and his wife and they were coming to sleep in there that night. Only two of them were in that ruined town.

When they had tried all their efforts to find us out but failed. Then they were coming back to that house with great anger when it was about eleven o'clock in the night and they were very happy when they met us sleeping in one of the rooms. When they entered that room and met all of us still sleeping, he told his wife to look very sternly at us with her big eyes. But she hardly did like that when the power of her eyes made us powerless at the same time. We were unable to move any part of our bodies but we could feel if something touched us and we could think as when we were not powerless by the power of the eyes of the hairy giantess.

Then as his wife did so, he first tied up our hands and legs with ropes. After that he put plenty of woods in the centre of that room and then lighted them. When the fire became powerful, he pushed every one of us nearly to touch it so that we might be roasted to death. Having done that he told his wife to take her eyes away from us or to stop to look sternly at us. But she hardly stopped to look sternly at us when we gained our power back. We could move and control every part of our bodies and then we were woken by the heat of the fire at the same time because we had nearly roasted to death before she took her eyes away from us.

Now, he and his wife sat in a little distance from us. Both were laughing greatly at us as we were in great suffering before the fire. After a while his wife put some pepper in that fire and as it was burning, we began to cough repeatedly. As our bodies were perspiring it was so our eyes and nostrils were watering and as we were shouting greatly for help it was so we were coughing and sneezing continuously and it was so both wife and husband were mocking and laughing at us.

After a while about two of us were fainted again and then we were three who were still shouting greatly with sorrow. But to our fear, these three men were hardly fainted when this fearful hairy giant and his wife walked to us and held them on heads and feet. They were preparing to put them in the centre of that big fire to be roasted and then to eat them. But luckily, before that time, the ropes with which my hands and feet were tied up, had dried up by the heat of the fire. So as they wanted to put these three fainted men in the fire, I was so feared that I stretched my body with all my power and then the ropes cut from my feet and hands suddenly.

Then without hesitation, I rushed furiously against them and as they were still holding the three men and were just lowering them into the fire, both of them fell backward suddenly as I dashed to them. The three men fell away from their hands at the same time when they were trying to save themselves from falling. And again, before they stood up, I ran to the corner on which his cudgel of stone was leaned and then I took it and again, without hesitation, I ran to the outside of the house. I hastily picked up my gun and got ready to shoot them to death when they came to me. And they hardly got up when they were running to the outside just to beat me to death at once. But as he and his wife were passing through the narrow door and as it was not contain both of them to pass out at a time. So their heads struck each other so heavily that they fell back to the house and the pains were so much for them that they were unable to stand up and then come to me.

So I ran to them and beat their arms with his cudgel until all were broken instead to shoot them with my gun. Then I hastily ran back to that room, I first took the three fainted men to the outside so that the fresh air might rush to them, and after that I ran back to the room, I cut the ropes away from the feet and hands of the rest men and then I helped them to the outside as well. All lay helplessly because they had nearly to die of heat of that fire. But as I was doing all this, the hairy giant was gaining his strength gradually and I hardly bent down just to examine the condition of those fainted men when he ran to me. He gave me a heavy blow suddenly and then I fell down a little distance away from him. But I hardly fell down when I hastily stood up and then I ran to him just to beat him in return. But it was a great disappointment to me that I was unable to do that when he gave me another heavy blow which landed me several times.

But as I believed that he would kill the rest men if I left them there and ran away for my life. So I ran to him again, but I started to wrestle with him this time. He tried to raise the whole of me off the ground and then to knock me to the ground but I did not give him chance to do that. After a while I held his right leg just to lift it up and then to push him backward but I was unable to lift it. It was so every one of us was trying all his power till about seven o'clock in the morning.

Before that time I had become so tired that I had no more hope that I would be saved. But as he was unable to knock me down, so he began to push me along to the extreme end of this hill, so that he might push me from there on to the big river which was at the foot of it. Having pushed me to the edge and as he pushed me to fall on that river. So I hastily held his neck with all my power and this prevented me from falling.

And he was still trying to push me on to that river, when Ajasa became conscious and then he ran to him and he pushed him suddenly and then he fell down with me. But as he was still struggling to stand up and then to revenge on us, we pushed him to the extreme end of the hill and then he rolled down on to the river at the same time. Having seen this, his wife, the hairy giantess, stood up and wobbled to us. But as she wanted to revenge on us, we joined hands together and pushed her on to that river as well.

As both of them were still struggling to save themselves from drowning, then we packed up our loads. Having helped the rest men to stand up, we continued our journey at the same time before the hairy giant and his wife saved themselves from the river. Having travelled far away from that hill and that we were quite sure that we were saved from them. Then we stopped and rested for some hours before we found some edible fruits which we ate. And within a few days, all of us were well. That was how we were saved from the hairy giant and his wife.

Then the people sang and danced for a while before they went back to their houses with great joy.

On the Way to My Village

The entertainment of the tenth night

Many special ceremonies were performed as the people of my village were drinking the palm-wine. Many lovely songs were sung and we danced together for about two hours because the stories of my journeys would be related to the end this night. But as we were still dancing and singing very loudly with great joy. The people were coming more and more from other villages to hear the rest story. Those who too old or too young to walk were brought by heads and shoulders.

After the drums were stopped to beat and we stopped to dance and sing, and everyone sat quietly. Then I continued to tell the last story as follows:

When we had saved from the Hairy Giant and his wife, the Hairy Giantess, who were the killers of the road of the town of wealths. Then we continued to travel along on that road. And within a few hours, we travelled about twenty miles before we stopped when we saw one hut a little distance from the road. But we did not see anybody in it nor we saw any sign to show us that the owner of it was coming in there frequently. Because there were spider webs all over the ceiling and several antlion pits were in every part of the corners.

So when we put our loads down, we made fire in the centre of the hut and those who had wounded and fainted in the house of the Hairy Giant, began to warm themselves with the heat of the fire. After a while, Ajasa and I went around that place. Luckily, we saw a big farm in which yams were planted. So we took as many as would sufficient for the whole of us, and then we came back to the hut. We roasted them and ate them to our satisfaction. It was like that we enjoyed our lives until those who had wounded were well.

We spent more than ten days in that hut with happiness but one midnight, after we had joked and laughed greatly, then we lay down and slept within a few minutes. And as we were still enjoying the sleep, we were woken suddenly by the great noise of a mad man. He held up one broken pot in which there was a big fire. The flame of the fire was so high up that it shone to everywhere. He hung a very big head of a buffalo on left shoulder and the blood was dropping down from it as he was shouting and coming to us, so this showed us that he had just killed that buffalo. There was a heavy stone on his head and one long cutlass in his right hand. He hung many fearful things all over his neck, waist, ankles, etc. He was half-naked and he was too fearful to see and his voice was too fearful to listen to.

And he was shouting terribly as he was coming to the hut as fast as he could: "Are you in there? How many of you in that hut? I am very hungry! Please wait for me!" Then with great fear all of us sat up and gazed at him as he was coming as hastily as he could. When he was at a little distance to the hut, he guided his eyes with right hand as he gazed at the hut, so that the powerful fire which he was carrying might not shine in to his eyes. He saw every one of us clearly when the fire shone to the hut. Having seen us, he was so happy that he began to jump up at the same time and was coming direct to us with great joy. But when he was about to enter the hut and as his attitudes showed that he was a real mad man and that he was coming in to kill us. Then we hastily took our loads and we began to run away in the darkness.

And without hesitation, this terrible mad man began to chase us along with the fire in hand. But when we believed that he would catch us soon, we scattered in the bush unexpectedly. Ajasa and I climbed one tree to the top and we hid there while the rest four men entered the deep hole of a big rock which was not so far from that tree. It was like that every one of us had tried to save his own life. As Ajasa and I sat quietly on top of that tree, we saw this mad man as he was searching for us with the flame of the powerful fire.

After a while, he saw the hole in which the rest men hid, but as he was entering it and as I believed that if he met them in there, he would kill them right out. So without hesitation, I shot him at back, but alas! my gun missed him and he did not feel anything on his back at all. Then having failed to disturb him from entering the hole, we began to whistle to them so that they might know that he was coming in to them. But we did not hear reply from them or any sign to show us that they heard the whistle. To our fear, after a few seconds that he had entered the hole, we began to hear the sorrowful noises and within a few minutes everything was quiet. We did not hear any noise again but we did not see neither our men nor the mad man to come out from the hole.

But as we were preparing to come down from the tree and then to enter the hole and see what had happened to our men. We saw him coming out with the heads of the men in his both hands. He had killed them. And then Ajasa and I bursted in tears at the same moment. To our fear again, as we were still weeping, he hardly came out when he began to look for us. After he had searched around there but did not see us, he began to look at the top of every tree which were near the rock. After a while he came to the tree on top of which we hid. He looked at the top of it for a few minutes and then he saw us when the flame of the powerful fire in his hand shone to our eyes.

Then he put the fire down and also all the heads of our men at the bottom of that tree. He held his cutlass firmly and then began to shake the tree with all his power. But of course, when I believed that if we came down, no doubt, he would kill us as well as he had killed the rest of us. So with fear, I shot his forehead and he fell down helplessly. Then we began to come down from the tree with the hope to continue to run away for our lives as before. But we hardly stepped down when he sprang up and he gripped Ajasa as firmly as if nothing had happened to him. Having seen him did so, I snatched his cutlass, I flung it far off and as he was trying to lay Ajasa down and then to smash him to death before he would come back to me. I hastily loaded my gun again and I shot his head for the second time. He turned round and then fell down but he still held Ajasa so tightly that he (Ajasa) was unable to take his hand back from him.

So without hesitation both of us began to pull the hand. But this mad man did not leave it until when he became conscious and then he was scrambling it with us as he was rolling here and there on the ground. At last, when we were unable to take Ajasa's hand back from him, I ran to his fire which was in a big broken pot. I took it and then ran back to the spot. I threw the whole of it on his head and breast. Then he felt so much pain this time that he released Ajasa's hand by force. And without hesitation, I took my gun and then we ran away for our lives. But I believed, he would die soon after we had left him because he was unable to stand up and chase us. But of course, the rest of our loads and the bows and arrows, etc. which the god of thunder had given us in Ede town, were in the hole of that rock together with the dead bodies of our men.

We ran as fast we could till the daybreak and then we stopped, we sat on a big insect mould which was on the roadside. Both of us began to think of the death of our four men. Having thought about them for some minutes, we continued to travel along on the usual road without eating anything, of course, we did not feel to eat and this was due to the sudden death of the men. And we came to the town of wealths when it was about five o'clock in the evening.

As we were travelling along in the town, we asked the first man we met to take us to the house of the chief and he took us to the house. We entered and met him in his sitting-room. He was among many people by that time but we waited until when he had finished with the people. Then we told him that we wanted to lodge in his house for only a few days when we would continue our journey. He asked whether we were looking for a job to do but we replied at the same time that we did not come there for any job but we come there to take from their wealths (all kinds of precious metals) to our village. He was greatly shocked to hear like that from us, but anyhow, he allowed us to lodge in his house. This town was very beautiful, gold, silver and diamond blocks were as common as sands everywhere in the town but the inhabitants did not recognize them as good things but they never allowed any body to take any of them away from there. But once the chief had heard from us that we come there to take some of their wealths away, he told their king and then they began to keep watch of our movements around the town.

One night, when the whole people had slept, I took one big gold block and I wrapped it with one bag and Ajasa did the same thing. But as we were leaving the town very cautiously, the dogs began to bark at us. They were barking so loudly that the people woke from the sleep and then they chased us to catch at the same time. After a while they caught us and we were taken to their king. And without any question, we were mercilessly beaten and the clothes on our bodies were torn into pieces before we were taken to their prison yard. But after my gun was taken from me and then the warders beat us for about one hour. We fell down and pretended to be dead then they left us and went away. Having noticed that they had gone away, we stood up, we entered the room in which my gun and the gold blocks, which we had been carrying away before they had caught us, were kept. So as our dresses had been torn into pieces and we were in nakedness this time, we first took some of the clothes which were hung on the racks in that room. We dressed up and then we took the gold blocks and my gun. After that we went very cautiously in the darkness to the wall of the prison yard and then with much difficulties, we climbed it and then jumped to the back of the yard.

And without hesitation, we started to carry the gold away although there was darkness. But when we were about to leave the town finally, a number of dogs recognized us again, of course they did not at the first instance because we had dressed up in the people's customary clothes. And when these dogs were barking at us again, the people woke up and were chasing us again to catch. And they were still chasing us along fiercely until we came to a river which crossed the road. As there were many canoes and paddles on the bank of this river, we hastily pushed one of the canoes on the river, we took two paddles, we put the gold blocks and my gun in it and then we jumped in it and then we began to paddle it along as fast as we could before the people rushed to the river.

But as we were still paddling along and as these people determined to take their gold blocks back and then to kill us. So they did not waste time but they pushed some canoes on the river and then they continued to chase us along to catch. Again, we did not paddle so far when we were seeing a deem light far away. So we were paddling the canoe towards it with the hope to hide in the house from which the light was penetrated to the river. But not knowing that there was no house at all. But that light belonged to a gang of the pirates. The light was in their mighty canoe and they were going about on that river just to attack the passengers who had valuable goods and then to take them by force,

But when we paddled our canoe nearer to their own canoe and we saw that they were pirates and again we noticed that there were many dangerous weapons, like long spears, bows and arrows, guns, etc., were in their canoe. We wanted to paddle our canoe back at the same time so that they might not attack us but the people of the town of wealths were approaching us nearer this time. Therefore, without hesitation, we paddled our canoe to the south of that river. Having seen this, the pirates began to chase us as well to attack us.

After a while, when they were unable to overtake us because their own canoe was very big and could not run as fast as our own. Then they began to shoot their bows and arrows and guns at us and after a few minutes they were throwing the spears at us repeatedly but we escaped into the darkness and by that we were saved from all the dangers.

After the people of the town of wealths had failed in all their efforts to catch us, then they paddled their canoes back to their town. But those pirates were still chasing us along with their canoe.

Having paddled our canoe hardly till the daybreak we came to another river. This river was very long and wide and its tides were very strong indeed. But we could not avoid all these troubles because the pirates were still behind and they chased until our canoe ran to the sea at the end of that river before they paddled their it back from us having failed to catch us.

And our canoe hardly entered the sea when we were unable to control it. After a while, the tides and waves broke it into two equal parts, our loads and the gold blocks were carried away by the waves, but my gun, hunting-bag and matchet were still on my shoulders. I lay flatly on one part of the canoe, I held it with all my power as it was carrying me far away on the sea and Ajasa lay on the second part, held it as it was carrying him far off as well.

It was like that both of us were parted without our wish. Two hours later, I found myself held up by the sands near one mountain. As I was craning at Ajasa to see whether he had drowned, the wave began to push him towards this mountain and after a few minutes, he was carried to where I stood. Having rested for a while, both of us thanked our Creator for saving us from all the dangers. That was how we were saved from the people of the town of wealths and from the pirates as well. But of course, it revealed to me at last that nobody could take the treasure (gold blocks) of that town away. People had told me about that long time, but I did not believe them.

Although we had saved from all the dangers but we were not so happy for we did not know what was going to happen to us again. We went around that place but there was no anything with which to cross the sea back to the bank. But when we went farther, we came to one spot and then we stopped there. And when I noticed it carefully, it was the very spot on which been held up by the sands when my canoe was split in pieces about two years ago when I had been crossing this same sea. When I noticed again, I saw the spot on which I made fire and I saw the barks of the plantains and yams which one of the attendants of the Goddess of Diamonds, sent to me when I was held up there. Now I was quite sure that this mountain belonged to the Goddess of Diamonds.

Then I began to tell Ajasa the story of the mountain, the Goddess of Diamonds and my former wife, Sela; who had followed me back to the village in my second journey but she was taken back to her town by the men of her mother, the Goddess of Diamonds.

So, Ajasa advised me to let us climb the mountain to the top. He said that he liked to see the Goddess of Diamonds and Sela, my former wife. But to my surprise, as we raised heads up and were still wondering at this mountain, there we saw that Sela was waving both hands to us, and she was laughing with great joy. But as we were about to start to climb this mountain to her. She waved hands to us to wait for her. So we stopped and then she disappeared among the trees.

After a while, she rode one camel to us through the same path on which that camel had travelled the day she had sent it to me. She hardly came down from it when she embraced me with great joy. Having left me she embraced Ajasa as well for she recognized him although it was quite a long time she had seen both of us. Having chatted for a while, she mounted the camel back and she asked us to mount it behind and we did so at the same time. But as she was riding it along, I told her that I would not follow her to her mother, the Goddess of Diamonds, because I was afraid not revenge on me. But she told me that her mother had become so old that she would not be able to recognize me again. Then I told her again that I would take her back to my village and to my surprise, she agreed to do so.

After a while, she rode to the town. Then she took us to her mother, the Goddess of Diamonds. She explained to her that we were looking for a job to do. And her mother engaged us as house cleaners. It was like that she deceived her mother.

Having spent one month with the mother and having taken plenty of the diamond blocks and hidden them far away from the town. Then I told Sela, my wife, to let us leave the town the following midnight and she agreed. Before then, she had packed all her dresses, she gave them to me to hide them for her.

Then in the following midnight, when she noticed that the rest people had slept. She mounted one of the camels and we sat on it behind her. She held one lamp as she was riding it along. When we came to the spot in which the diamond blocks and her dresses were hidden, she stopped the camel.

We put them on the camel and then we continued our journey. And we had reached the sea and entered the canoe as well before the daybreak. Having travelled for about two days on the sea, we came to the village. So my mother, father, brother, sister and friends were very happy to see my return. And all were wondered greatly to see that I was so bold and brave to bring my former wife, Sela, back once more. But it was a great sorrow for the families of four of us who had been killed by the mad man in the hole near the town of wealths.

It was like that we went to the underground and returned. After a few days, I gave one part of the diamond blocks to Ajasa and I sold the rest to the merchants who dealed in such precious stones. So I became a rich man since that day and this my wife (she stood up and posed herself to the people as I pointed finger to her) and I are living comfortably!

"Now, my people, that was the end of my journeys. So it is very scarcely to go on a journey and return without punishments, hardships, etc. etc!"

Then the whole people shouted greatly with joy and then stood up. We sang and danced together for one hour before they went back to their houses. And I was recognized by all the people of the village as the chief of the village since when they had heard my adventures of the past days.